cw

W0007908

© Italiaander

Published by Delancey Press Ltd
23 Berkeley Square
London W1J 6HE

www.delanceypress.co.uk

Copyright © Gary Italiaander 2014

The right of Gary Italiaander to be identified as the author of this work has been asserted by him in accordance with the Copyright Design and Patents Acts of 1988. All rights reserved under International Copyright Conventions. No part of this publication may be reproduced, stored or transmitted in any form or by any means without prior permission in writing from the author. Reviewers may quote brief passages.

A CIP catalogue record for this title is available from the British Library.

First published 2014

Jacket by Italiaander Productions

Cover Design and portraits by Gary Italiaander

Typeset by Italiaander Productions

Printed and bound in the UK by 4edge Ltd

ISBN 978-1-907205-25-5

Dedicated to the memory of
LARRY ADLER

ACKNOWLEDGMENTS

I would like to thank all those who have helped to make this tribute a reality. I began the process shortly after Larry's death, and I am delighted that so many contributions have come from his family, friends and those that had the privilege of making music with him.

In particular, I want to thank my wife Tamar for her support without which this book definitely would not have seen the light of day. In addition, a huge thank you to my daughter Elise who has recently entered the world of publishing. She has been in the perfect position to assist me with the editing. Last, my parents for their continuing support and particularly my father, who has created illustrations where no photographs exist.

"Once the harmonica is in my hands and ready to play, it immediately loses its identity and becomes instead, an orchestra with strings, woodwind and brass and a rhythm section with me both as conductor and player."

Larry Adler

Quote from Accordion Times and Harmonica News, Feb 1936.

CONTENTS

FOREWORD

Why this book?

This is something I cannot easily answer.

That I felt a compelling responsibility to create a tribute to Larry Adler is without question.

His talent inspired me as I had displayed musical ability at a young age. Music is still a passionate interest to me although my work has taken me in a different direction. I have been fortunate enough to meet many interesting celebrities through my work as a portrait photographer but Larry was the one person I always wanted to meet and photograph. Not only did I get that opportunity but an amazing friendship developed as well.

We had shared interests; we both loved music with the ability to create it. It's just that his ability to do so was in a different league to mine! I would not be so presumptuous as to compare my musical talent to Larry's in any way but that unquestionably had a bearing on how our friendship developed and my need to create this project.

We also shared a love of tennis. When I first met Larry he was still playing occasionally and when I asked him if he won, his reply was; "I never win!" Somehow, knowing the man, I doubt this was the case and I feel sure that, at least in his younger days, he was rather good.

We did discuss creating a book together but at that time Larry wasn't able to make a commitment as he was already in his early eighties - still travelling, performing and busy with the writing that he was doing for a variety of magazines. He did however provide a number of opportunities for me to create a photographic record. The reason for making such a record was unclear at the time, but I felt it was important to do it all the same. The significance became apparent once he'd departed the stage, with the concept for this book.

While Larry was in hospital in London, seriously ill, he received an invitation to perform in a concert at the Royal Albert Hall for Prince Phillip's 80th birthday. He was told by his doctors that he was far too unwell to attend (to which he agreed); nevertheless, he slipped out of the hospital and made his way to the venue. Only when he appeared on television were the medical staff aware that he had done so. No matter what his state of health, it was always Larry's view that 'the show must go on!'

At the time of his funeral I was abroad, but I was invited by his family to attend the memorial concert that took place at The Arts Theatre in London some time later. During that concert, when his family, friends and associates spoke of him, it became clear to me that I should gather together thoughts and comments from those who knew him personally and so I began collecting memories from those closest to him. However, for a variety of reasons, I became aware that it was the wrong time to complete this project.

Two of the most important people in Larry's life were his brother Jerry and Larry's partner for the last eighteen years of his life, Gloria Leighton. Jerry was delighted to be able to put something on record. Gloria was more reticent as she was unsure whether she had the ability to write but she eventually agreed (with lots of encouragement from me). This was only on the basis that my wife, Tamar, would do all the typing for her and I am extremely grateful that Tamar agreed to do so. Gloria had a lot to contribute, as you will, and so I am delighted that we were able to capture her own very special thoughts. It is fortunate that I started the process when I did as sadly both Jerry and Gloria are no longer with us.

Once I realised the 100th anniversary of Larry's birth would be in 2014, I decided that it was time to complete the project. Nearly everyone I have been able to contact has agreed to participate. I am delighted that I have been able to gather so many contributors who have added their own 'reflections'.

This book provides a brief history of Larry's life, interspersed with my own commentary, as well as tributes from his family, friends and associates. What clearly emerges is that Larry was the greatest of entertainers, perfectly at home performing on the mouthorgan (as he preferred to call it rather than the more usual harmonica) or as a raconteur, speaking and joking with his audiences. His approach to performing remained the same, regardless of what had happened or how he felt.

So, I now feel that I have achieved what I set out to do, creating this tribute. Larry; although in many ways he appeared down to earth and quite ordinary, he left his mark on our world in the most extraordinary way. I am honoured that he allowed me to share some memorable times with him that I can now share with you, along with those reflections of his family, friends and colleagues.

The Dream

It was early morning, 6th August 2001 when I awoke from a dream.

That may not seem particularly unusual, except in my case I am rarely aware of dreaming (even when they have taken place) and even less likely to remember them.

The dream, though quite short, was as follows:

I was visiting Larry Adler at his flat. He greeted me at his doorway. Yet it didn't look as I knew it to look; there was a stairwell behind me spiralling for many floors. Larry's building had a lift. Although I found this strange, I accepted the change and extended my hand towards him. The next thing I knew, I was falling backwards down the stairwell. Larry, who stayed in view throughout my fall, appeared to get smaller and smaller until he was just a speck in the distance. Then I woke up.

I didn't think too much of it, and so started my day. At the time, I was in France with my wife Tamar, and my children Elise and Simon. We were staying with friends at their home in the Loire Valley.

Later that day, while having lunch in their delightful French chateau, I received a call from another friend, Chris, back home (in London) to let me know that it had just been announced on the radio that Larry Adler had died.

Chris was aware of our friendship and didn't know if I would hear the news where we were. I was extremely upset and also shocked by this. I had not been aware that Larry had been so ill, as I had not seen him for a while.

I then remembered the dream of that morning and was left wondering whether Larry had literally 'dropped in' to say 'goodbye'?

So how did I get to meet Larry Adler?

When I was about six years old, a cousin gave me a harmonica that nobody used. I picked it up and could play it immediately. My whole existence was taken up with this little instrument that I could take everywhere with me. At an early point I became aware of the name Larry Adler – if for no other reason that at least one of the harmonicas I had acquired was called the *Larry Adler Professional.*

That in itself is an unusual story and one that Larry was interested to hear about, along with the following:

I was born in London and at around the age of three I contracted Tubercular Meningitis. To survive such an illness in the late 1950's was in itself something of a miracle but to do so kept me hospitalised for a year. Fortunately I have no recollection of this at all. But having been so ill, and for such a long time, a check-up was essential twice a year in the form of an X-ray. On one of these visits, we had to pass a very large music shop called Squires. They sold just about every instrument going and on this particular day, I was stopped in my tracks by the sight of a mouthorgan in the front of their window. It was simply stunning; I had to have it!

When I got home that night I was so excited that I could not wait to tell my father about it. I must have been about nine years of age at the time. My father listened with great interest and then asked me what I would be prepared to do to enable me to get one. He asked whether I would kneel on the ground and kiss the floor. That seemed an odd request although at the time, I didn't question it. I answered that of course I would if it would get me the instrument. He then asked me to demonstrate that I would in fact do so. I did.

When I stood up, there on a plate (on the table) was the mouthorgan that I had seen that very morning. Imagine my astonishment! By a strange coincidence my father had also seen the instrument in a different music shop in Central London where he worked – Chappell of Bond Street. He had bought it there and then. While I was telling him about the harmonica, unbeknown to me, he actually had it in his pocket and so was able to perform this 'miracle'! I was speechless, probably for some time, and of course I was over the moon!

The Larry Adler Professional 16 Chromatic Harmonica - still in my possession over 50 years later. © Italiaander

Sometime later the head of my school, who happened to also be a musician, spotted my musical talent and called my parents in to talk. He wanted to know if they were aware that I had musical ability and if so, had they considered what they might do to help with my musical development.

After taking piano lessons for a while, I sat a music exam and became what is known as a 'Junior Exhibitioner'. This entitled me to attend a London Music College under the guidance of Dr W S Lloyd-Webber (the father of Andrew).

Since first becoming aware of, and transfixed, by this amazing little instrument that would fit in my pocket, I have been a fan of Larry Adler. So much so, that it was my dream to meet him, although there was no valid reason why this should ever happen.

I studied music, and after some years (including studies in America) I qualified as a music teacher and became involved in music as a career. However, after some time my passion for photography took me in a new direction.

I started to work professionally in my new chosen field. Some years later, I received an answerphone message from no other than a certain Larry Adler. I was both surprised and delighted to receive this call but to my extreme disappointment, it was not the Larry I was hoping to meet. By coincidence, this Larry was the agent for another musician – Peggy Seeger (the sister of Pete).

However, it was following my change of direction into photography that I first had the opportunity to meet the Larry

Adler that I had been hoping to meet.

In 1995, having just opened the Italiaander Portrait Gallery at Harrods, I was invited with my wife Tamar, to a Variety Club lunch at The Dorchester Hotel where Larry was to be one of the celebrity guests. The event was for the comedian Davy Kaye who had devoted his life to helping disadvantaged children through the Variety Club. Another guest who was there to speak about Davy was Dr Christian Barnard (who carried out the world's first heart transplant).

During the lunch, the lights dimmed, an orchestral (recording) started and suddenly Larry was performing. It was a magical moment!

After lunch, I was introduced to Larry by John Ratcliff who had invited us to this special occasion. John, a past international president of Variety and his wife Marsha Rae, (who had created Gold Heart Day which has raised millions for the charity) sang my photographic praises and told Larry that I wanted to photograph him.

Larry gave me his phone number and invited me to call him to arrange a portrait session. I did so the next day and he suggested that I drop by, there and then. Fortunately I had some free time and to my amazement I discovered that his home was a short walk from my studio in Primrose Hill. We met and arranged what was to become the first of a number of portrait sittings.

I was looking forward to having the opportunity to photograph Larry and spend some time talking about music. I didn't for one minute expect that we would develop a friendship, but Larry often dropped by my studio. We would meet for lunch or I would occasionally go to concerts where he was performing and take some photographs. Subsequently I photographed him a number of times – in his home, in my studio and on stage.

Larry with Gary Italiaander (and sculpture by an American artist) at the home of Cindy Lass. © Italiaander

Larry's Early Life

It is not my intention to write a complete history of Larry's life as he did that in his autobiography, *It Ain't Necessarily So,* which makes fascinating reading!

Larry as a young child Joachim Kreck Film - und Fernsehproduktion

But I will at this point talk about how Larry started on the road to becoming the most unique presenter of the harmonica of all time and dip into that history periodically, to give some perspective to when certain things took place.

Larry started his autobiography with an explanation of his choice of the title, pointing out that memory is open to interpretation. He did this by talking about an incident involving him, which had occurred in Germany. A few different people had recalled a story as they remembered it and all the recollections were quite different. Larry then began to question his own memory of the event!

Deciding on the most appropriate title for this book, *Reflections – A Tribute to Larry Adler,* was relatively straightforward. Just as it was, when I decided to write the book in the first place. I wanted to collect a variety of memories about this remarkable man and to create a lasting record.

At the time of writing *Reflections* it had been difficult, and in some cases almost impossible, to obtain a clear record of certain information, particularly regarding tennis. However the most important aspect, his musical life, has been documented here by those who knew him well.

For now, let's go back to 1914, the year Larry was born.

Lawrence Cecil Adler was born on the 10th February 1914 in Baltimore, USA just before the outbreak of World War 1 - a fact that he hoped someone in the future would consider to be significant.

It is fair to say, although no one would have been aware of it then, he was about to make his mark on this world.

Larry was born into a Jewish family; his parents, whose original family name was Zelakovitch, were born in Russia before moving to America as infants.

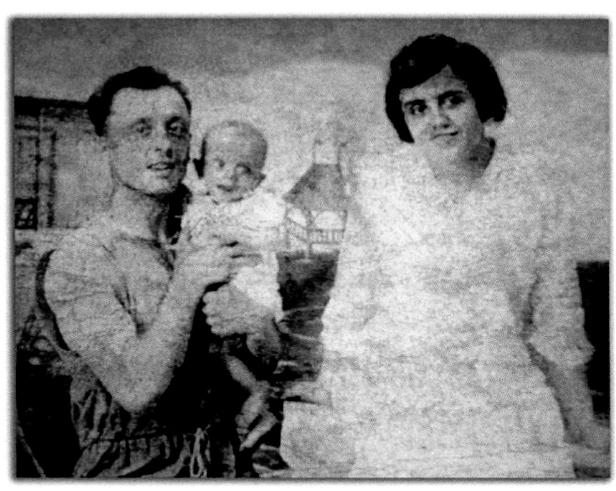

One of the earliest portraits of Larry with his parents.
From Larry's private collection - with kind permission of Marmoset Adler

As a young child, no one in Larry's family was musical, but when he was around 5 years old an uncle took him to see Rachmaninov perform in Baltimore and Larry was immediately smitten. After this, Larry was taken to see Al Jolson perform and he then wanted to be a combination of the two - Al Rachmaninov!

Larry's father ran a plumbing business and Larry would sometimes help with plumbing jobs which convinced him, whatever his future, it did not include a career in plumbing.

Larry's brother, born five years later, was named Hilliard

Gerald but was known as Jerry. He also went on to become a harmonica maestro in the USA like his older brother.

A young Larry

With kind permission of Joachim Kreck Film - und Fernsehproduktion.

Jerry Adler

Written shortly after Larry's death in 2001, during Jerry's visit to Britain for the Memorial Concert. Jerry was also a harmonica maestro, mainly performing in the USA and on cruise ships. He died in 2010.

Now, my recollection about Larry. At the age of 10 he became the junior cantor of our local synagogue in Baltimore. He was a tyrant about mother, dad and I following the rigid rules of Sabbath. No lights in the house except for candles. We were forbidden to carry money in our pockets which, unfortunately, was not a terrible sacrifice because we didn't have any!

When Larry was 10 years old, he was walking down the street in Baltimore and suddenly passed a music store. He was fascinated by a beautiful Mason-Hamlin piano displayed in the window. He walked into the store with the assurance of a knowledgeable adult that he was seriously interested in the piano. Word has it that the salesman, in his eager desire to make the sale, promised Larry that if he was serious about the purchase, he would throw in a Hohner chromatic harmonica!

Larry eagerly ran home to inform our parents that it was his dream to own this exquisite piano. Dad was a hard-working plumber who eked out a living that bordered on poverty. He actually talked Dad into going with him to see the piano and then the salesman talked our father into making the purchase. Larry promised that he would dedicate his life to learning the piano. But if the truth be told, I believe that he was far more interested in the "free" harmonica!

When Larry decided to pursue show biz he was determined

to not break his orthodox rules on kosher food and proceeded to eat corn flakes three times a day. This went on for over three months until he began to gag on this popular cereal. Larry definitely made the break with a vengeance which included shrimp cocktails, ham sandwiches, Chinese pork dishes ... the list goes on. I can only assume that this fall from grace provided the excuse to chuck Judaism completely!

His lust for the opposite sex came at an unusually early age. Having entered the arena of glittering lights, his fascination with the entertainment business seemed to be fused with the excitement of working in theatres that included a line of very attractive chorus girls. He did lie about his age, claiming that he was 16, which seemed to have gained acceptability with theatre owners throughout the country.

His pursuit of the opposite sex was quickly out of control and at such a tender age, (14 if I'm not mistaken) he had a string of conquests that boggled the mind.

He was not particularly attractive. Short, scrawny and terribly near-sighted with his horn-rimmed coke bottle lenses that seemed to emphasize his physical deficiencies. Yet, his ability to get himself involved with the most beautiful women remains one of the great mysteries.

The ensuing years solidified his ability to find the most alluring sex goddesses which became legend. However, he has allowed some of these women to literally walk all over him with the tiresome excuse that he "didn't want to hurt their feelings." These same women were unmerciful in their desire to wrest his considerable wealth from him.

Jerry Adler © portrait by Italiaander

.

Larry and I were not interested in athletics so his interest in music started at the age of 12. That's about when he became fascinated with the "mouthorgan." We are both self taught due to the characteristics of the instrument. I do not know, nor have I ever known, of a good teacher so it was up to us. We were 5 years apart in age and I was inspired by his genius and I pursued the instrument with great energy.

In his ever-consuming desire for sexual pleasures, Larry became the easiest "mark" around. He protected the "integrity" with his ill-conceived belief that they were honest and all they wanted to do was to protect his welfare.

Larry was well into show biz when I began to teach myself so he was not around to give me pointers. I have always worshipped him as a musical genius but more so as a very loving brother.

Our father was a hard-working plumber and mother was a well-organized homemaker, adoring mother and excellent cook.

When Larry became enmeshed in the disgrace of the McCarthy hearings, it totally destroyed mother and she spent the last 35 years of her life in and out of mental hospitals.

There is no doubt that Larry was an original in the world of classical music who proved to a world-wide audience that a simple instrument, the harmonica, in the sensitive hands of a true artist, can achieve the respect and admiration accorded to musical giants such as Vladimir Horowitz and Isaac Stern. I vividly recall a rehearsal at the Hollywood Bowl where there was to be a concert with the Los Angeles Philharmonic featuring Horowitz, Stern and Adler. Larry who played the piano with some virtuosity had the chutzpa (cheek), while the audience was having a break, to start playing the piano in the presence of *musical royalty.* Horowitz said to him; "Larry, why do you continue to play that silly little instrument, the harmonica? THIS is your instrument!"

But there is no doubt that Larry's instrument was indeed the harmonica. He gave me the love, understanding and encouragement to make it my instrument as well, allowing me to establish my mark as a solo performer.

By coincidence, I have officially retired from the music business, and on November 6th I gave my final concert here in Sarasota. I plan to donate my harmonicas to a local high school. 68 years in the business is quite enough. I am now 83 and intend to live out my life in peace and comfort with my dear wife, Jean.

I have never been as devoted and as dedicated as Larry was in his pursuit of musical success. He has achieved the kind of successful heights that we all dream about. However, he paid a heavy price for it.

Larry begins his career

Eventually, it was decided that Larry would be given piano lessons. Enrolled at the Peabody Conservatory of music in Baltimore where he studied the piano, he achieved the distinction of being the only student to be expelled from the Peabody! He had prepared a waltz by Grieg and as he entered the stage the Principle said; "And what are we going to play little man"? The 'little man' didn't like being referred to in this way so instead of playing the Grieg he played *'Yes, we have no bananas'*! Following this, his parents received a letter stating: 'Do not send him back!'

That was effectively the end of Larry's academic music education. A little while later, he had seen in the *Evening Sun* newspaper that a harmonica group was being formed so he went along to see what it was like. There was a man there who had been sent over from Germany by the Hohner harmonica company to form a band and teach the harmonica. Larry liked him and could see that he was a natural teacher.

After about a year of lessons, the *Evening Sun* sponsored a competition, which Larry entered and made it to the finals. The main judge for the competition, Gustav Strube, was the founder of the Baltimore Symphony Orchestra and while all the other boys played popular songs, Larry played a classical piece; the Beethoven Minuet in G. At the end of the competition, after conferring with his panel, Gustav stepped forwards and announced:

"Ve haf given de avord to Lorenz Cecil Aidler mit an average of ninety-nine und nine tents." He shrugged, apologetically. "No von is pairfect." (Larry Adler; *It Ain't Necessarily So,* 1984).

While growing up, it was a time of great bigotry and according to Larry the ethnic groups feared and despised each other and they avoided each other. He personally experienced anti-Semitism but didn't understand the logic behind what made people think that way.

Star Harmonica Artist, 15 To 'Do Stuff' at Century

Lawrence Adler, 15, City College graduate and former Peabody student, who is a harmonica soloist on the Loew's Vaudeville Circuit, will make his first professional appearance in Baltimore next week at the Century.

He was a star of the City College Glee Club and also played in many amateur events until he went to New York and made a prompt hit on the professional stage. At Peabody he was a student of piano. With the harmonica, however, he developed his own technique. One of his best numbers was Gershwin's "Symphony in Blue."

Adler's engagement here is for one week. He will then continue his tour of the Loew circuit. He is a son of Mr. and Mrs. Louis Adler, 2200 block Bryant Ave.

Lawrence Adler

With kind permission of Joachim Kreck Film - und Fernsehproduktion

Larry wanted to leave home and go on the stage and as he had managed to gather around $50 from subscriptions of a magazine that he sold (which his parents didn't know about), he did just that. Astonishingly, at 14 years of age, he simply bought a ticket and took a train to New York. Once there, he phoned his parents to let them know where he was and they immediately went to get him.

However, he told them that if they did take him home he would simply run away again. He didn't want to go back to school or to Baltimore. His parents consulted the family doctor who said that he was a very neurotic child and therefore the best thing was to leave him alone and let him stay in New York. Larry believed that the doctor hoped never to have to see him again.

When Larry first got to New York, all he wanted to do was get a job on the stage in vaudeville. At this time the harmonica was considered to be a child's instrument. A friend managed to get him an audition with 'Borah Minevitch and His Harmonica Rascals' who were the biggest name at the time where the harmonica was concerned. Larry played the same piece that had won him the competition in Baltimore but when he finished playing, Minevitch said, "Kid, you stink"! Larry was extremely upset, burst into tears, and his first thought was to go back to Baltimore. However, once he'd had time to think, he decided to try elsewhere and managed to get an audition with Rudy Vallee who at the time was a huge star.

Vallee gave him the first opportunity to get on the stage at his night club and so Larry stayed in New York. Within a week he landed a job with Paramount, touring all over the United States on a salary of $100 a week in 1928, which is roughly the equivalent of over $1,300 today. This tour gave him the opportunity to learn stage craft; in particular how to entertain an audience as he was performing up to six shows a day.

Larry had an amazing level of 'chutzpah'. Whatever an obstacle came along, he found a way to overcome it. Even when he couldn't get work or things weren't going so well, he remained confident in his own talent.

At the age of 15 he was effectively 'kidnapped' off the street by a well-known gangster who was married to the singer, Ruth Etting. He drove Larry to the studio where Ruth was creating a record and insisted that Larry be included in the recording. She tried to object but clearly that was not an option and the band, which included Benny Goodman as well as Jimmy and Tommy Dorsey, agreed to put him on the record.

That same week, Paul Whiteman was playing in town and so Larry hung around the stage door and whenever he saw someone about to enter he would play in their face, hoping that someone would say 'what a talented kid' and give him a job. Whiteman's saxophone player, Frankie Trombauer, liked what he heard, led him into the dressing room and told Paul to listen to the kid.

He played a popular song and when he finished it, Whiteman said, "...play the *Rhapsody in Blue*." At 15 years of age it was technically beyond his ability but he wouldn't admit that there was anything that he couldn't play so he replied, "I don't like *Rhapsody in Blue.*"

Whiteman then turned to a young man that Larry hadn't noticed before who was sitting at the piano and said, "How'd you like that George?"

And that's how Larry met Gershwin!

Larry auditioning for Paul Whiteman - the first meeting with George Gershwin

© Illustration by Michael Italiaander

The relationship between the Hohner Company and Larry Adler by Clayman B. Edwards – CEO of Matth. Hohner AG.

I believe that Hohner's early advertisements for harmonica's *'Don't be a loner, get a Hohner'* describes the beginning of a life-long relationship between Larry Adler, the greatest harmonica player in the world, and Hohner. At the age of 13, Mr Adler entered a harmonica contest sponsored by the *Baltimore Sun* and was awarded a silver cup as first prize. Having been thrown out of multiple schools and with a passion for the harmonica, Mr Adler ran away to New York in 1928 to audition with *Borrah Minevitch's Harmonica Rascals,* a top vaudeville act at the time. Unfortunately, Minevitch told him he stank, but undeterred Adler stopped by the Paramount Theatre where Rudy Vallee gave him a chance and so the story begins of a talented and motivated man and an instrument of inspiration, the Hohner harmonica.

In 1934, Adler held his first appearance in London. By 1935, Hohner had introduced two Larry Adler chromatic models for international sale. Adler's music had driven Hohner's sale of harmonicas to England to increase by two thousand percent in a single year. Larry Adler's worldwide influence on the popularity of chromatic harmonica playing sold millions of Hohner harmonicas and inspired generations of players.

During the 1940's the Larry Adler model chromatic harmonica was the largest selling instrument in the world and the team of Adler and Paul Draper became one of the highest paid concert attractions in America. It was Adler's amazing gift with the instrument and in promoting his music, his friendships, and his collaboration with Hohner that propelled him to become the greatest.

As for Larry Adler's friendships, his letters to Hohner and his statements in the media illustrate his mastery of talking about himself, revering his many high profile friends, and making you feel like you are just as important in the conversation. In one letter to Hohner's Marketing director, he writes, "Now I am organizing an 80th birthday album. George Martin will produce. Sting and Elton John have volunteered to appear on it. I only want artists I know personally. How's your singing voice?" In a casual name dropping contest with Walter Cronkite, Adler mentions that Charlie Chaplin called him in Beverly Hills and asked him to come and make up a foursome for tennis, Bill Tilden's dropped out. So Adler arrived and Chaplin motions for me to get on the court. Not long thereafter, Adler learned that the woman badly dressed for tennis was Greta Garbo and the man with the weird moustache was Salvador Dali.

Larry Adler's sole goal in playing the harmonica was to develop a 'singing tone'. He said, "If you can get a singing tone in your playing, that's as far as you can go. Miles Davis does it on the trumpet; Johnny Hodges did it on the saxophone. That's what I loved about Rachmaninoff when I heard him play the piano when I was a kid in Baltimore. Years ago, I played *Sophisticated Lady* with Duke Ellington and his band at the club. Billie Holiday was there and afterwards Duke introduced me to her at the table. She said, "You don't play that thing, Man, you sing it." Now I cannot think of a better epitaph than that."

The Hohner Company is extremely proud to have had such a lifelong relationship with Mr Larry Adler. He made our mouthorgans sing and he became the pied piper of his generation.

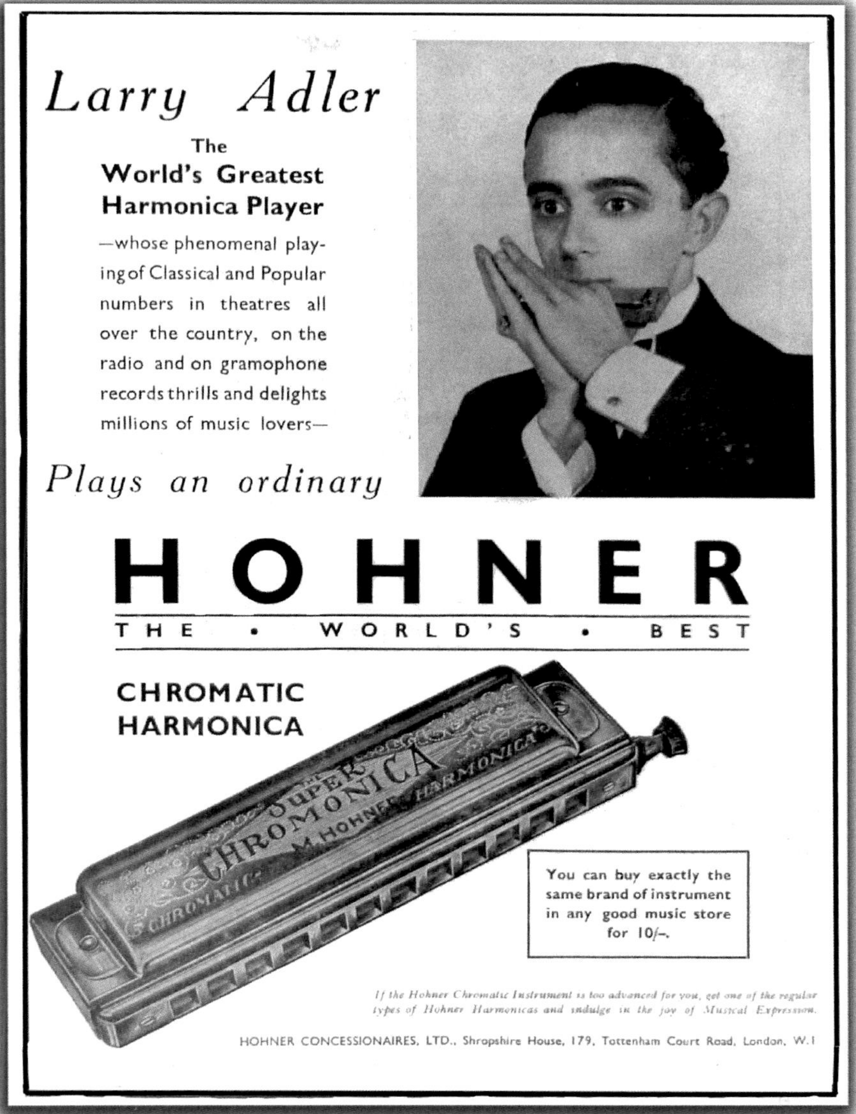

Larry Adler: Brilliant ambassador of the Hohner-Chromonica - Classical harmonica soloist of world-class calibre by Arnold Kutzli

The harmonica is played in over 140 countries worldwide. But what if it hadn't been for the musicians that gave this little musical instrument the voice it deserved. Creativity, ingenuity, virtuosity, as well as persuasiveness were the most important factors here.

The company founder Matthias Hohner chose his slogan to be "my field is the world", and this attitude was to lead to many a win-win situation in the company's long history.

The example of 'Mister Harmonica Himself', Larry Adler, makes this especially clear. He must have been the most famous harmonica soloist of the 20th century; he made the harmonica fashionable. In this context one should point out the CD, *The Glory of Gershwin* he recorded for his 80th birthday together with Sting, Elton John, Cher, Kate Bush and many others. Adler's masterpiece then: *Rhapsody in Blue*.

It is remarkable that the marketing of Hohner-USA itself contributed to Larry Adler's interest in the harmonica in the first place. Already as a little boy in Baltimore he won his first competition. He was the only one who chose to perform Beethoven on the harmonica; an absolute novelty. No wonder that at the age of 14 he was already at the beginning of his stage career.

The year 1930 was a benchmark for Larry Adler. It was the beginning of a lifelong connection to Hohner in Trossingen, the city of the harmonica. With this, he had established himself as an advertiser for Hohner.

"There is only one Chromatic HARMONICA
the HOHNER
THE WORLD'S BEST
says Larry Adler

This heyday of his artistry was dominated by performances ranging from Swing to Classic; amongst other things, he played as a soloist accompanied by a symphonic orchestra. It was therefore all the more painful to see him 'blacklisted' during the McCarthy era, thus practically banned from his profession - an unbelievable decision.

It went quiet about Larry Adler and surely this was partly due to the change in people's musical taste. However, this made the World Harmonica Festivals that took place in Trossingen in 1989, 1993 and 1997 all the more impressive: there he was performing again, the world-class musician with his unmistakable charisma.

So until this day, even beyond his 100th birthday, Larry Adler and his Hohner-Chromonica mark a milestone in musical history. A history, this exceptionally gifted musician has co-written.

Arnold Kutzli initiated and organised the World Harmonica Festivals in Trossingen, as well as the World Music Festival in Innsbruck. He was Procurator and Director of Culture Marketing in the Matthias Hohner AG, Germany.

(Translated from German by Verena Rechmann)

Dr Antony Dannecker

"I have always felt honoured, but humble, when working with such a genius as Larry Adler".

All top concert artists, whichever instrument they have mastered, require the backup of technicians with the experience and technical ability to maintain the instrument being used with a consistency of all its working parts, while enabling the artist the opportunity to create the best sound.

Antony Dannecker & Willi Dannecker, Hohner's Chief Mouthorgan Repairers in Europe, tuned and maintained Larry Adler's harmonicas from the early 1950's right up until his death in 2001.

"Due to Larry's busy performing, recording and touring schedule, his collection of harmonicas were in perpetual need of tuning and adjustment. Over these 50 or so years, I guess Willi and I must have completed more than 4000 of these overhauls to his three octave chromatic harmonicas".

"When my mouthorgans are out of tune I need Antony Dannecker, who besides being Chief Hohner Repairer, is also my friend".

Larry Adler

The War Years

In 1943 Larry's agent, Abe Lastfogel, was made head of the USO - The United Service Organization, providing live entertainment to US troops at military bases within the United States and overseas.

Larry was invited to participate and jumped at the chance. In fact, even though he was booked to perform for a number of weeks in Chicago, he lied and said that he had been drafted for an overseas tour which allowed him to get out of the commitment.

Once the USO tour was announced, Larry was contacted by the founder of the Chicago *Sun* to see if he would do a weekly dispatch for the newspaper. As he had always been keen to write, this provided the perfect opportunity and it was agreed that his fee would go to The Red Cross.

It gave Larry the opportunity to travel widely all over the world entertaining the troops with Jack Benny and a host of other stars.

It was during one of these tours that he first met Ingrid Bergman. Although married at the time to his first wife, Eileen Walser, it didn't stop them from forming a close relationship with Larry considering whether his future was to be with Ingrid.

Working on this project has unearthed some fascinating images from the period and I am extremely grateful that the holders of the images made them available for use with this publication.

Larry with Ingrid Bergman, Jack Benny and US servicemen

Larry with Ingrid Bergman on the balcony of the Reichskanzlei in Berlin 1945, Martha Tilton can be seen below.

With kind permission of Joachim Kreck Film- und Fernsehproduktion

Close-up of the previous image – Ingrid can be seen photographing Larry

With kind permission of Joachim Kreck Film - und Fernsehproduktion

During this visit to Berlin, Larry played *The Battle Hymn of the Republic* while Ingrid recited the Gettysburg Address.

This, one of the most famous historical U.S speeches, was delivered by President Abraham Lincoln in 1863, during the American Civil War, at the dedication of the Soldiers' National Cemetery in Gettysburg, Pennsylvania, soon after the Union armies defeated those of the Confederacy (at Gettysburg).

Jack Benny with Larry Adler – extracted from documentary film

With kind permission of Joachim Kreck Film - und Fernsehproduktion

A remarkable photograph!
Ingrid Bergman, unknown officer, Jack Benny & Larry.
Taken in the room in the bunker where Hitler committed suicide.

With kind permission of Jonathan Shalit

Larry had commented on occasions (and in his autobiography) that he considered himself a coward. I don't know whether he really believed that to be so but things that happened to him and his response to these happenings indicate that this was not the case.

One example of this refers to The Hohner factory - producer of the world famous harmonica, based at Trossingen in the Black Forest, Germany. During the war, being a German factory they were forced to work for the German war machine. At one point, Larry found himself based near Stuttgart on an overseas tour which was close to the Hohner factory. He didn't want to pass up the chance to get some new instruments; by this stage it had become a French-occupied territory but getting permission to travel to the area would have taken some time. A pilot, hearing of the situation, told Larry that he was prepared to take him there immediately in a small plane he had access to. This was not easy as the war was still on. However, when they located a suitable place to land in a field nearby, they did so and were soon surrounded by French soldiers. It just happened that one of the soldiers played the mouthorgan, knew of Larry and escorted him to Hohner. The trip was a success and two senior members of the Hohner family who there at the time, were delighted to see him. He left Trossingen with many new harmonicas - or mouthorgans as Larry preferred to call them.

The second, and very definite example of Larry's strength of character refers to the dreadful period of American History known as McCarthyism.

In brief, it was brought about by a real fear of Communism. Once Senator Joseph McCarthy introduced the concept that there was a real threat to US security caused by Communism, it started a ball rolling that caused great damage to many people, a number of whom ended up committing suicide. The FBI, under the leadership of J Edgar Hoover, also helped to develop the idea that many people needed to be side-lined, particularly in the entertainment industry. An advertisement from the period shows just how seriously this matter was taken as it was considered a danger to the American way of life.

AMERICANS.....

DON'T PATRONIZE REDS!!!!

YOU CAN DRIVE THE REDS OUT OF TELEVISION, RADIO AND HOLLYWOOD.....

THIS TRACT WILL TELL YOU HOW.

WHY WE MUST DRIVE THEM OUT:

1) The REDS have made our Screen, Radio and TV Moscow's most effective Fifth Column in America . . . 2) The REDS of Hollywood and Broadway have always been the chief financial support of Communist propaganda in America . . . 3) OUR OWN FILMS, made by RED Producers, Directors, Writers and STARS, are being used by Moscow in ASIA, Africa, the Balkans and throughout Europe to create hatred of America . . . 4) RIGHT NOW films are being made to craftily glorify MARXISM, UNESCO and ONE-WORLDISM . . . **and via your TV Set** they are being piped into your Living Room—**and are poisoning the minds of your children under your very eyes ! ! !**

So REMEMBER — If you patronize a Film made by RED Producers, Writers, Stars and STUDIOS you are aiding and abetting COMMUNISM . . . every time you permit REDS to come into your Living Room VIA YOUR TV SET you are helping MOSCOW and the INTERNATIONALISTS to destroy America ! ! !

From Wikipedia

Having lived in America in the late 60's when I was a teenager and at High School, I was aware of the very strong anti-communist comments (that I heard in school) but felt that this had nothing to do with understanding what Communism was actually about.

Larry documented exactly what happened to him and how it affected him personally in his autobiography. He was required to say whether or not he was a Communist and to name others that he knew were Communists, neither of which he was prepared to do, whatever the outcome for himself.

He spoke to me about how terrible a period this was and the damage it did to many of his friends - all huge names in the world of entertainment. Like many others, Larry was 'blacklisted' and this meant that he could no longer work in America – people simply would not or could not offer him employment.

Fortunately, he was already well-known internationally and what was happening in the States was of little interest abroad. When he was invited to visit London by C B Cochrane, who was the major name in entertainment in the UK, the opportunity was too good to turn down and Larry made London his new home.

He rebuilt his life and continued to be a huge force in the world of music and entertainment, until the end of his life.

Larry's passion for tennis

What it was that originally captivated Larry's interest in the game of tennis has not been possible to discover and unfortunately, it was a question I never thought to ask him!

However, it was an interest that grew into a passion that led, it seems, to his playing every day where it was possible to do so.

One of the earliest and best known stories is about how Larry received a phone call from his friend Charlie Chaplin inviting him to join a doubles game that had been arranged as one of the players had dropped out at the last moment. The person unable to make it that day was none other than a certain Bill Tilden who, with his incredible record, is considered one of the greatest players of all time; he won the Wimbledon title three times and held the position of number one player in the world for seven years.

Larry with Chaplin, Garbo and Dali. © Illustration by Michael Italiaander

On arriving at Chaplin's house, Larry was ushered onto the tennis court but did not immediately recognise the other two players. After a short while it became clear who they were; Greta Garbo and Salvador Dali - an incredible mixture of characters.

According to Larry, Chaplin was the best player there with incredible anticipation.

Larry enjoys a game in the sun
From Larry's private collection - with kind permission of Marmoset Adler

Larry proving that you can make music while playing tennis. He commented, "… this is probably why I never won Wimbledon!"

From Larry's private collection - with kind permission of Marmoset Adler

Living in London provided the opportunity to visit Wimbledon on an annual basis for the world famous tournament and Larry was often seen in the player's box.

On one occasion, Larry was invited by Virginia Wade to join her on court but he wasn't keen to be shown up. "Don't worry" she said, "I'll make you look good!"

With Wimbledon winner Virginia Wade
From Larry's private collection - with kind permission of Marmoset Adler

Once Larry became known for his writing, he was invited (and paid) to review tennis as well. This included visits to such places as the Lew Hoad Tennis Camp in Mijas Costa, Spain. Two weeks with his daughter Marmoset at the club, with all expenses covered. At the end of the period, Larry would then write his review.

Larry was a member at the Paddington Tennis Club and often played with his close friend, Victor Lownes, who headed Playboy Europe and the UK Playboy clubs.

Larry had Hohner make some very special miniature mouthorgans inscribed with his name and gave them as gifts. These are fully functioning instruments and in the image above he demonstrated that you could really produce a tune on them.

The most special was the 24 carat gold version (above), reserved for the most special occasion such as winning Wimbledon!

Anyone for tennis?

From Larry's private collection - with kind permission of Marmoset Adler

LARRY ADLER: FOOD and HUMOUR by SALLY CLINE

I was married to Larry Adler for a decade and after the divorce and several tough years I was his friend to the end of his life.

Larry with his second wife, Sally Cline
From Larry's private collection - with kind permission of Marmoset Adler

He brought an extraordinary gift of music into my world, along with three magnetic, interesting and occasionally challenging stepchildren: Carole, Peter and Wendy (who sadly has since died) and later our own delightful daughter Marmoset.

In the early years Wendy was away in New York but Peter, also a fine musician, lived with us in the London house when he was home from Dublin University. With his return came more music, more young men, loud, cheerful, each playing a different instrument, all of them hungry.

Eileen, my stepchildren's mother lived round the corner and I always remember that when due to visit her for lunch, Peter would hastily remove his habitual creased jeans and tacky t-shirt and slip into a smart suit and even a tie for the visiting hour. Sometimes I wondered: what did Eileen have that I didn't in relation to bringing up kids?

Carole, of the three my closest friend, from the start, and still today, also lived close by, until she moved to the States. I saw her frequently and we would laugh about Larry's awful quirks, especially his egotism. The elder kids, who called him PAF (Poor Aged Father) rang him regularly. Carole would report that the first two thirds of any call would be taken up with Larry recounting his successes, concerts, record sales, and promotional events, then he would say he loved them (which he certainly did) and would be about to hang up. At this point the child in question would say; "How about me PAF? Ask about me?"

All Clines and Adlers shared a sense of humour and a love of food. Those characteristics, mine subtly British and his loudly American, were the main supports of our household. I sometimes think it was our Jewish background, our similar sense of wit, and a shared love of borscht and smoked salmon that kept our marriage going when many seemingly cogent factors signalled that it should have fallen apart.

Laughter and the joy of eating bonded us early. Indeed our relationship started with a Jewish soup joke. In my former role as a journalist with the once glossy journal *Queen,* I went to Edinburgh to interview this famous classical harmonica player who had just begun to divert his artistry into a one-man-show. Not classical at all! I had been told he was exceptionally gifted. He was. I had been told he was extraordinarily egotistic. He was. I was determined to remain unimpressed. Nobody however, had told me he was extremely funny nor that he adored food.

I sat down quietly at the back of the modest fringe theatre where he was performing. I remained unmoved, and cynical. Then between virtuoso pieces on the mouthorgan, he told a story.

'A customer at a Jewish restaurant in New York is so well known as a borscht lover that whenever he comes to dine, the waiters immediately serve him borscht without bothering to take his order. One day after being served, he calls the waiter over.

'"Waiter" he says, "taste the borscht."

"You don't like it" the waiter says anxiously.

"Taste it!"

"Look, you don't like it, so I'll change it."

"Taste it" says the customer patiently.

"Why do I have to taste? You don't like? So, I'll give you a menu, you'll select something else. I'll bring already. And no extra charge! We only want to please you."

The customer grows angry.

"*Taste the borscht!*"

"Look, I got 57 other customers here. I'm gonna taste everybody's borscht? I won't get any work done."

The customer stands up and leans over the waiter.

"Will you *sit down* and *taste the borscht.*"

The waiter sits down. He looks round the table. Then he says: "So where's the spoon?"

The customer, satisfied, says "Ah, *hah*!"'

I laughed until the tears streamed from my eyes. Then I went backstage and interviewed him. It was not love at first sight, it was laughter at first hearing. It was genuine identification with the worst and the best of my upbringing and with food as a medium for humour.

We went out that night and shared the first of many meals. Some were hilarious, some quietly joyous, some bitter, some painfully sad.

"So where's the spoon?" became a key to the code between us. A code that at some fundamental level never broke, despite a divorce, despite many passing decades, despite Larry's death.

A version of this anecdote was first published in: *Just Desserts: Women and Food.* (Andre Deutsch. London.1990)

Memories of My Father by Katelyn Adler - known affectionately as Marmoset

My father Larry Adler requested that any contributions at his funeral were either musical or humorous. This was not easy for me in my state of sadness about his death so I chose to read out a poem he had written for me on my 30th birthday. It was funny and it felt good to open the service with words written by him.

I think my first memory of my Dad is of when we were abroad in a hotel. I must have been about three years old. He was in the hotel bathroom shaving. He could not hear me calling his name so I walked in there and slipped on some water on the floor and broke my leg. I remember yelling in the hospital for him to stop the doctors hurting me. When we arrived back at the airport in England with my Dad pushing me in a wheelchair, my mum looked as if she was going to faint. My Dad had not told her that anything at all had happened to me.

When I was growing up I was often introduced as "Larry Adler's daughter. A friend of my parents' once said to me that he thought that what was unique about my Dad was that not only was he the best at what he did but that he was very likely to be the best there ever would be at what he had done. That struck me as being very likely to be true.

What I know about being a principled person and standing up for what you believe in I learnt from my father. He chose not to name names during McCarthy's blacklisting era. He

Marmoset plays a duet with her dad
From Larry's private collection - with kind permission of Marmoset Adler

refused even to read out a list of names already given to the House Un-American Committee. He did not recognise their right to ask him the question of whether he was or was not a member of the Communist party or indeed any questions. Friends of his became unable to work as a result of being blacklisted. Some committed suicide. My father went from being one of the highest paid performers in America to being without any means of earning a living. He was at the time married to an English woman and so he came to England with their three children. He lost his respect for America over the blacklisting and he never regained it.

I was not born until many years after this series of events but I feel it has shaped who I am as a person. Being principled is not an easy route to take in life. It can be exhausting and not just for the person making the stand. It is exhausting for those around them. And I realise we can't always take the hardest route. Sometimes we have to decide what issues we will let go. That too can be hard. I often refer to him in my head prior to deciding what to do about a decision that feels hard to make. For years I think I made my judgements about people based on what I thought my Dad would have thought of them.

During my childhood my father told me that if any member of staff at my school ever hit me he would have the school closed down. I believed he was all-powerful. I knew that his love was unconditional. I felt that very deeply. I knew that if I was ever in trouble he would stand by me and help to get me out of it. I knew there was nothing I could do that would lead to him abandoning me. That made me feel incredibly secure. It is a feeling I have tried hard to instil in my own two extraordinary children. When my father died, one of the things that struck me was that if I got into any trouble from this point on, I would have to bale myself out of it. That was a very scary feeling.

Throughout my life, when we would speak on the phone, I would remind him near the end of the call to ask how I was and what I had been doing. It would not have occurred to him to talk about anyone other than himself. I genuinely always found this strangely endearing and amusing. He was unlike anyone else that I knew. He had had a fascinating life. He had met almost every famous person anyone could mention. He had been in show business from such a young age that his education had been cut short and yet his intelligence and his knowledge outstripped others with many more years of education than him. He read all the time – fiction, non-fiction, newspapers and magazines. He was always writing letters, articles and reviews. He loved good conversation that he was at the centre of.

I have no memory of my parents living together. The time I spent with my Dad was often just with him, always based around his work and often abroad. I would go to his show and there would be drinks afterwards and then we would go for dinner. As I grew older I kept a whole section of clothes that I only wore for events that I went to with him. We talked a lot. He was very affectionate. He was incredibly funny. I loved the way he told jokes. I never tell jokes because I don't think I can tell them as well as he did.

My Dad never cooked. In his kitchen he had coffee, tea, cornflakes, milk and honey. Every meal we ever had together was from somewhere else. We usually ate at restaurants. He was a restaurant reviewer for several years and he was very fond of anything free. Free meals became a fixture. It was great to be able to try many dishes without feeling pressured about wasting the money that they would cost. Eating out felt like a very liberating experience.

Every year on my Dad's birthday Peter Stringfellow would host a birthday party for him at his club. The bunny girls would serve the drinks and canapés. Peter would give a speech. At the end we would stay for a meal. My Dad had a lot of meals there. He was never embarrassed about accepting such freebies. He loved them.

Around the time of my 30th birthday I flew to Australia to see my Dad perform at the Sydney Opera House. I bought a red silk dress to wear and I sat in the Royal Box. My father told the audience his baby had flown all the way to Australia to see him perform. Everybody clapped. It was lovely. When I was ten he and I went to Kenya for four weeks where he was performing each night in a nightclub. When I was 19 I went with him on the QE2 where he was performing. I never tired of watching him play or listening to him talk. Interestingly, I didn't even tire of hearing him tell the same jokes over and over. I think this may have been because he was so good at telling them. I genuinely really liked and admired him as well as loved him.

My Dad was in hospital once and when the nurses went to check on him he had disappeared. As the nurses watched the television screen in the corridor they saw my father performing at a concert in honour of Prince Philip at The Royal Albert Hall. They could not believe he had managed to escape without them noticing. I am not sure if that was an example of his work ethic or his bloody mindedness. It made me laugh a lot.

My Dad was a terrible driver. His treasured Alpha Romeo Spider was covered in dents. He refused to wear a seat belt in case the doors became locked following a crash and he became unable to get out. He had numerous parking tickets ripped up by officials who were charmed by his wit, his name and the free tiny mouthorgans he carried with him.

Marmoset surrounded by images from Larry's private collection
© Portrait by Italiaander

My father was crazy about tennis. During the many years that he knew the head grounds man at Wimbledon, Dad had a seat actually on centre court. All the players had to pass him as they came on and went off the court. The BBC worked out one year that the person who had been most filmed of anyone that season, including any of the players, had been Larry Adler. That pleased him.

My Dad did not know how to be part of a conversation. He only knew how to be the centre of it. He would sit and hold court at a party and people would gather round him to listen. I am not sure this is good for a person. I assume it was because he had been famous from such a young age that he did not know how to behave socially in the way most other people do, or at least he was not interested in learning. I think he genuinely believed he was the most interesting person in the room. And sometimes I guess he was.

I never tired of hearing my father play. His music was exceptional. I was always proud of him, always proud of being his daughter. He was not a traditional father but he was the right one for me. I have no hang ups about him and no regrets. We had many good times together. I travelled all over the world with him, ate lots of meals together, hung out in his flat in Chalk Farm together, we were affectionate towards each other. There was nothing that I wished afterwards that I had done differently and that felt good.

Some additional images from Larry's private collection

Larry with Marmoset

Preparing mouthorgans

Preparing the next generation of mouthorgan players!

Gloria Leighton was Larry's partner for the last eighteen years of his life and her story makes fascinating reading. After Larry's death, I had the chance to get to know her better and it was my persistence that led to her finally putting her thoughts about their relationship on paper.

She was particularly concerned that she was not a writer and would only do so by speaking into a dictating machine that my wife Tamar would then transcribe into print. As Gloria did this over a period of time, there were often random thoughts that she made clear, and it would be my job to edit later.

I am grateful that Gloria made the record and for her valuable contribution. I know she would be delighted that this project, in Larry's memory, has been completed.

Gloria Leighton © Portrait by Italiaander

Larry Adler - Off the Record by Gloria Leighton

I suppose, in a way, I'm hoping that being persuaded by Gary to write for this tribute that it will be a cathartic exercise for me because I'm not used to the fact that the telephone won't ring again (with Larry at the other end).

So, where do I begin? This is simply an insight of the man I knew as opposed to the famous artist known worldwide.

I was married for seventeen years until 1974 to a wonderful man, Leon Leighton, and my marriage was as near to perfect as a marriage could be. I was proud to be his wife. We had one son, Edward, and since Leon was a very hard act to follow, I had not remarried when Larry came into my life nine years later in 1983.

It is perhaps a coincidence that I write this first paragraph on September 11, 2002. How devastated Larry would have been to see his beloved America so needlessly attacked. He would have wept for his homeland despite living in London - since the disgraceful McCarthy period in American history - it was that which brought him to these shores in 1949. America's loss was our gain. His proclivity was to the left but never was he a card-carrying communist and I always felt that he was hurt, rather than bitter. He told me there was a very good reason he had never joined the Communist Party: "You know I could never take orders!" I knew that to be true.

The man I knew was a complex character in many ways. A living legend. In the millennium year, he was named on a list of 100 of the most famous people of the past century.

I am unaccustomed to accosting men – famous or infamous – but, on this occasion I plead guilty.

Sometime before that fateful cruise when it all began I had met Angela Buxton, the 1956 Wimbledon winner of the ladies' finals with Althea Gibson, and also that year runner up in the ladies' finals. The name Leighton meant something to her as two of my late brothers-in-law were very active at the Chandos Tennis Club and Richard had, in fact, found the site for the Club.

"I often give parties, give me your telephone number and I'll invite you next time", suggested Angela. We are still very good friends after 20 years. The first party I went to included a guest – one Larry Adler – to whom I did not speak to all evening as I was doing rather well in another direction with somebody who offered to take me home not knowing I had brought myself by car. However, on the way out I passed Larry and asked, "What in your opinion is London's best restaurant?" He said "Tante Claire" without so much as a smile.

The next time I saw him was on the QE2 - first night Captain's Cocktail party. I was on a five and a half week holiday with my friends Gary and Dolores Rosen when I saw him drinking alone in the crowd and on impulse I said, "I'm going to say hello but I'll be back in a moment because I think he's an old grouch!" With hindsight I think had I said 'do you remember me' he would perhaps have looked the other way, but I chose the more logical opening line - I believe we have a mutual friend. He was then charm personified and I could not too easily get away, so I said, "I am with friends, would you care to join us?" After the party we went to dinner and then we took lunch and dinner together for two and a half weeks until his contract expired. He asked me to leave the ship with him in Honolulu. I declined since my holiday was planned - one week Hong Kong on the QE2, then the USA West Coast to San Francisco.

I was not exactly a pushover! The first night on the QE2 he escorted me from the dining room and later (as he thought) to my cabin, but when we got into the lift I pressed my deck number and, as I got out, pressed for him to go on his way. He afterwards told me that he felt emasculated (actually he said "it was a balls-crushing experience!"). I kept it that way until the last night when after two and a half weeks he said, "may I have the honour to see you to your cabin?" So gracious a request I could not refuse and ...

The next morning he rang me for the first time and said ... "I'm on deck, it's 9 o'clock and already I miss you ..." that was my first dose of Larry the Charmer ... nevertheless he disembarked in Honolulu and I played a little harder to get, until later when we were both once again in London.

Larry and I met, eighteen years before his death and enjoyed a wonderful, albeit, turbulent relationship. My respect for his talent is immeasurable. We all know his music but how did he develop so brilliant a brain and rapier wit with no formal education? He was elected a fellow of Yale, invited annually to the debating societies at Oxford, Cambridge, Durham and other universities. He spoke on panels with Bertrand Russell, AJP Taylor and other such luminaries. Wyoming University retain his archives. In many ways we were diametrically opposite but we dovetailed in that his was the great brain and mine the everyday common sense and business acumen.

Together we had a great love of the English language and fervently hoped that one day it would be sanitised to exclude all cliché's. He was a great friend and inspiration to many, and took a firm stand when any issue came under the heading of "rough justice". His spelling was, I think, without error - he was like a walking dictionary and thesaurus combined and what disagreement we had could often be purely semantic.

Many times Larry was accused of name-dropping but I never felt that about him. His life was filled with other celebrities - an endless roll call of famous stars, royalty, aristocracy and even those in the gangster world. Virtually ninety percent of the people in his life (literally) were well-known names, so I don't ever consider he was name-dropping; he was just telling it as it was.

When we met on the QE2, where he was entertaining on board, I had a pretty good idea of his persona and could see that without subtle manipulation, his autobiography would never be written. Perhaps "bring me a chapter each time you want to see me", was not so subtle but it worked and by 1984 the book was published. We were invited by

Collins to a meeting in the country to launch the book. Forever, I shall remember the Chairman (or Sales Director, I am not sure which) saying; "Without this lady you would not have this book to promote". My pride when he presented me with a small gift, a souvenir; a hand painted porcelain trinket which has sat on my dressing table ever since, was immense.

I followed what the press described as the longest engagement on record - his eight-year on/off with Lady Selina Hastings. I guess I got him on the rebound!

In many ways, he was an enigmatic character - many facets to him, very endearing, a self-acknowledged lovable slob, which is why I could never have married him. We lived a different kind of life. We existed on the cut and thrust of a very turbulent relationship. We thrived on it in fact. Together we had no great need for other people. We spent most of our time simply enjoying each other. Yes, he was a womaniser and the odd woman here and there could be forgiven because we needed each other and always, no matter what, he would pick up the telephone and we would pick up the pieces again. I really think it was this breaking up and making up that kept us going - stupid and juvenile though it may sound, it worked for us. I was in a semi-impregnable position; somewhat indispensable yet occasionally temporarily disposable!

The first time we were invited to a Hope Charity event (by Gary Italiaander), Larry went on stage and played 'Jerusalem the Golden'. He played with so much emotion; his rendition was so moving that I think we all drowned in an emotional silence when he finished. Usually, he would say something before and after he played a piece, but in that instance, he just stood up and played and sat down again. It was one of the most moving performances I can ever remember and one of the most memorable evenings. Larry raised countless thousands of pounds for charity simply by giving his services free of charge and his name to guarantee a ready sale of tickets.

On board that ship he asked me one evening, "Liv Ulman and her daughter are on board. They're giving a party, will you come with me?" Also on board were Lord Lichfield and Vic Damone. I thought it was rather odd to go to a party where I hadn't been invited. I soon realised that to be on Larry Adler's arm, I was welcome at any party (and what a great life it was!) especially at the beginning when he was a food critic; not only did we have the most exotic meals in the most wonderful restaurants but with total red carpet treatment.

Larry was much more sensitive than one would imagine. One anecdote I think that always moved him to tears was during the six day war in Israel when he visited a young man who hadn't spoken or shown any sign of recognition, was probably semi-comatose for a very long time, and after Larry played he suddenly was aroused to join the land of the living again.

He always fought for what he felt was right. He had very strong principles. Nobody could move his line of thought once he had made up his mind, as when Salman Rushdi was going to speak, Larry said he would attend. Before that particular meeting, Larry received a death threat but he was not deterred. He appeared and lived on but that was the sort of man he was. His word was his bond and he really never let anybody down insofar as a concert or an appearance was concerned. His agent, Jonathan Shalit, often said that whereas many younger performers would cancel for some reason or other, Larry always went through with any sort of commitment.

So far as the public were concerned, when asked for autographs, he was always polite and pleasant - the only thing that rather irritated him was if somebody put a book in front of him without a pen. In his later years, when he was suffering very seriously with gout (which was in his right hand), he was terribly apologetic if he was unable to write.

'Second Hand Rose'

He was not the most romantic man insofar as sending flowers or birthday cards or the little niceties a woman appreciates, but having said that whenever he received wonderful floral tributes from friends and colleagues like Sir Elton John, Sting, Lord Bragg... they would come to me. Thank you, all of you who sent Larry fabulous flowers over the years. I enjoyed them immensely!

His music for the film 'Genevieve', was so much admired. Most people knew that he played during the film but not many were aware that he actually composed 'Genevieve'. Sadly, when he was nominated for an award for that composition, due to the McCarthy era his name was not allowed to be on the credits in America and the award went to Muir Matheson who had simply conducted the orchestra.

Many years later, a young man who knew about this, made it his objective that Larry should receive the award, which ultimately he did.

One of his best friends who was absolutely wonderful to him was Peter Stringfellow. Peter gave Larry a super birthday party every year.

Another great friend whose home we visited many times for parties was little Davy Kaye and I say little advisedly, because he was one of the few people I could almost tower over. I remember a special luncheon that was given for him at the Dorchester when Dr Christiaan Barnard spoke warmly about Davy Kaye. It was very touching. That afternoon I sat next to Frankie Vaughan, who was Deputy Lieutenant for Bedfordshire.

He was at one time a good friend, or much more (I'll never know how much more) with Ingrid Bergman and together they made a fantastic recording, she speaking the 'Gettysburg Address' and he accompanying her with the 'Battle Hymn of the Republic'. It was a very moving piece and I often said to people, "...well, Ingrid Bergman is a very hard act to follow!" The answer I got from one of my friends was, "...yes, but you're still making the chicken soup!" To my amazement when he died, the obituary in the Daily Mail mentioned my name in the same paragraph as Ingrid Bergman - something I thought I could never aspire to!

Larry was not a great one for flattering and I learned not to expect it. I was very pleased when I was told by so many people that all the lovely things he should have said to me,

and he answered, truly and in Adleristic fashion, "I don't want courtesy, I want class!"

The day before he died, I awoke at 3.45am, rested a while then suddenly felt impelled to go to him. I arrived at the hospital at 6am and stayed for six hours, heartbroken and frustrated because he was unable to speak to me - didn't know I was there and I so much wanted to tell him not to leave me, rather like the song from Camelot; *If ever you would leave me*. Sadly I returned home and at 6.45am the next morning, I called the night sister who told me sorrowfully, "at 2.30am ..." I know that when Larry died, part of me died with him. That in his mixture of genius and celebrity there was also a childlike innocence which played to my maternal instinct as well as the more usual and obvious emotions.

Random Thoughts and Memories

Larry's talent could be summed up in three words – GIFTED, GENIUS and GREAT. There is not and never will be another artist whose name is synonymous with the instrument he plays. As a crossword clue or a quiz question, his name is the answer.

He was invited (I believe the only American in an all British programme) to the Queen and Prince Phillip's 40th wedding anniversary. I had the pleasure to be there also - a small gathering in the Arena at Earls Court. I was in the front row bordering a gravel path where each car stopped and the passengers alighted - a very thrilling event.

I have a photograph of Larry with the Queen Mother taken in a room at Clarence House - also standing by is Lady Soames. 'The Queen Mother has hold of Larry's instrument' (as he tells it). She had a wicked sense of humour and said, "I didn't think I would ever hold Larry Adler's organ in my hand!" I've no way of verifying this comment and it may come under the heading of his autobiography, *It Ain't Necessarily So!*

More recently I had the pleasure of meeting the Right Hon Sir Nicholas Soames and offered to make a copy of this delightful photograph to send to him. I have in return a very charming letter from him dated February 2001 saying how touched his Mother was to see it.

Entertaining HM The Queen Mother
From Larry's private collection - with kind permission of Marmoset Adler

During our long relationship, Larry came very near to marrying another and I had a written proposal from a very elegant man in New York, twelve years younger than Larry and very personable. I flew to New York to be sure of my feelings. I arrived on a Friday and returned on Tuesday because for me the magic was not there. Although Larry had feigned indifference, he was ringing my bell the evening I arrived back. I said, "How did you know I was home?" and he said, "... because I drove by every evening to see if your light was on". So much for indifference!

Forty years ago he wrote a book *Jokes and How to Tell Them* and nobody told them better than he did. He very much liked one-liners and for some time, he liked to open with ... Eve said to Adam, "do you really love me" and Adam replied, "Who else?" I told him that particular joke; I remember where and when but he was reluctant to acknowledge that!

There was nothing machismo about Larry. He might boast about that in which he excelled but was quite content to admit to being dumb in certain other respects. When we saw a TV or cinema film, I often arrived at the denouement long before he did which earned for me the soubriquet Miss Marples Leighton.

He was by no means an inveterate liar, rarely even white lies, easy to see through because he was an unimaginative one. For example, he knew I would never be the first to telephone after a spat - I might get a call to say, "My line has been out of order, did you call me?" Like hell I didn't! Or late night standing on my doormat with those spaniel eyes and a hangdog expression; "I can't find my front door keys". Depending upon my mood it would either be, "Oh well, come in", or he would go into orgasmic shock when I chose to give him a set of spares, which I always kept.

When we were visiting Australia and New Zealand in 1995, there was an Aboriginal dance exhibition staged in the open air, which some years later I saw performed before the Queen and Prince Phillip. Larry was so admired by them because they knew he was sympathetic to their cause, the reclamation of their land. It was incredible that they knew and so loved and respected him. This dance exhibition was solely for Larry (no other audience) and when it was over we were invited in the time-honoured custom to rub noses with each of them. Also while in Australia, we met and dined with Wing Commander Michael Parker and his wife. He was a friend of Larry's and a friend of very long standing and Equerry to Prince Phillip.

Larry was very knowledgeable and always totally au fait with American politics. He was, of course, a democrat. He had great insight and not long before he died, chanced to remark to me that one day it would be acknowledged that former President Jimmy Carter was one of the greats. He was so right. Sadly he did not live to see this confirmed when Carter became a Nobel Prize Winner.

Parties

Most parties we went to were buffet style. Larry had an unwritten law NEVER to select his own food. He would sit down and hold Court and why not; people were flattered to be with him and he could be interesting, funny and flirtatious. Ca va sans dire that I was always the food carrier. Imagine, I am 5ft tall; I must first battle my way through crowds to get to the table, decide what my 'Master' would like to eat, then forage my way through a mass of people holding the plate aloft so that it would be an indication of my plight. I would arrive seemingly like the periscope of an invisible submarine. My prayer would be that he didn't want a second helping before I had to repeat the process for his dessert!

Tennis

Apart from music and women, there was another great love in Larry's life - tennis. His story of playing in a doubles match with Charlie Chaplin, Greta Garbo and Salvador Dali, he told many times over. That was long ago but his love for tennis continued throughout his life and when age caught up with him, he said he played "Cinderella tennis" - he never got to the ball!

He was a member of the Paddington Tennis Club and played often with Victor Lownes, a great friend of long standing. He would tell me when Victor got mad at him he would call him, "You no good Commie bastard," all in good fun. Other members I met there were Martin Amis and Timothy Haas. Through his friend Alan Chalmers he enjoyed many privileges at Wimbledon. Occasionally I was with him. It was always the Competitors' Box and the NBC tent for lunch. One year I sadly missed was when Cary Grant was there.

He knew Virginia Wade and often told the story of how she played down her game so that he came out seemingly a better player than he really was.

In the last year or two of his life, it was too much for him to go to Wimbledon - walking was difficult and stairs became his enemy. Instead he had to be content to watch TV. Not quite the same as the electric atmosphere of actually being there.

He enjoyed the privilege of being allowed to play on the tennis court of the home of the US Ambassador at Winfield House, Regents Park. In the last year of Larry's life the Ambassador was named Lader; curiously an anagram of Adler.

Piano

Larry was originally a student of the piano at the Peabody Conservatory in Baltimore. I simply loved to hear him play piano; his harmonies were pure Adler.

I was with him in Baltimore when a new Hotel was opened - the Peabody Hotel - which boasted "The Larry Adler Suite". In Baltimore I met one of his favourite pianists, Ellis Larkin. Larry was always generous in his praise for those he admired and appreciated. In 1999, when he was yet again invited to Australia, Andrew McKinnon introduced him to a brilliant young classical pianist, Simon Tedeschi, who was then eighteen but had at the age of nine his debut at the Sydney Opera House and aged fourteen was the "hands" of David Helfgott in the Academy Award winning film "Shine". Larry was ecstatic and described him to me as a “young Rachmaninov.” Since Larry had grown up with Rachmaninov as his idol, this was praise indeed and I could not wait to meet this wonder boy. He called Larry “Pop” and Larry called him “Son” and they were great together.

Larry with Simon Tedeschi
From Larry’s private collection - with kind permission of Marmoset Adler

When Larry opened a concert, stepping out from the wings with the strains of the verse of “summertime”, slowly advancing to the piano to play keyboard with one hand and harmonica with the other, this thrilled the audience and had to be seen to be believed. Sadly, in his later years when gout affected his right hand, he could no longer stretch an octave so could no longer perform this wondrous piece of pure magic.

Yes, magic could describe his artistry, a dynamic virtuoso, compellingly charismatic, unique, mercurial and sometimes, oh so fiendishly goddamned irritating!

During a Sting concert at the Royal Albert Hall, Sting asked Larry if he would perform *Shape of my heart* with him on stage. Larry was concerned that he wouldn't be recognised by such a young audience. Therefore, he agreed to walk onto the stage unannounced during the piece when he would start to play. A roar went up from the young audience. Following *The Glory of Gershwin* recording, he had become a cult figure - evident by the number of young people at the stage door when the concert ended and the rush for autographs.

That was THEN and this is NOW ...

On New Year's Eve in 2001, I was in the Honours List, having been awarded an MBE. January 1st was a day of joy and sadness. Sad that neither my late husband nor Larry were here to share this with me. The award was instigated by my very much treasured life-long friend Martin Shaw, to whom I am eternally grateful, and Larry had submitted one of the five referral letters which culminated in the award. I know he would have been overjoyed for me. Larry gave me honest and sincere encouragement when I considered to counsel for Crisis Counselling for Alleged Shoplifters.

Although involved in various social work for many years, I thought counselling could defeat me but Larry simply said, "You don't know your own potential and I know you can do it". I have been with the Registered Charity, of which I am an Executive Counsellor and Trustee, for seventeen years. This, plus hospital work, children's Country Holiday Fund work etc. culminated in my award, so to a degree, once more "thank you Larry".

Andrew McKinnon - a wonderful friend to us and still a much treasured friend to me - it was he who arranged for me to travel as a VIP in 1995. 1st Class is great but if you haven't experienced VIP, then MAN YOU AIN'T LIVED!

I so much enjoyed the company of June Mendoza, superb artist. Her triptych (not three panels but three in one) portrait of Larry, just fabulous and is a preface illustration in his autobiography. She was a great hostess at parties in her Wimbledon home.

Others I met at Larry's birthday parties: the colourful and somewhat eccentric Marquis of Bath ("... darling, please do call me Alexander"), Peter Sissons and his delightful daughter Kate, *News of the World's* Stewart Kutner, Martin Bell, Alan Jay Lerner, Henry Mancini, Marvin Hamlish, Gloria Hunniford, Wayne Sleep, Angela Rippon, Cher, Ernie Wise, David Soul, Chris de Burgh, Tony Bennet. Having been kissed by Tony Curtis (Ritz party Paris), Charles Aznavour at a Covent Garden Party. The radio names – Kevin Howlett, Ken Russel, David Jacobs,

Malcolm Laycock, Desmond Carrington, and on and on … like a shopping list.

More random thoughts

At the memorial service for a well-loved theatrical agent, I found myself sitting next to Joss Ackland, who invited me to share his Prayer Book for the final hymn - so I can claim to have sung a duet with him! Behind me were two celebrities debating, when it would be their turn to be the star of a Memorial Service.

Berlin

Again, with Jonathan and Issy in the very beautiful Schlosshotel designed by Karl Lagerfeld. Décor so elegant, it was no surprise that one afternoon we saw the Duchess of York – not staying there but looking in with obvious appreciation of all she saw.

Japan

On the QE2 we visited China and Japan. Larry was very proud of the fact that he was given a sartorial fortune by way of several outfits by the renowned Issey Miyake. He loved to convey this to an audience and the accordion pleated dinner suit he wore for Prince Phillip's 80th birthday concert, was a Miyake masterpiece - unfortunately, not seen at its best because Larry was in a wheelchair. Larry always said that in Japan he was regarded as GOD, which I think would be confirmed by his fan club.

All the years Larry lived in London (since 1949) he was, of course, a Labour supporter. A friend of Neil and Glynis

Kinnock, he was invited to the annual grand fund raising dinner. That last time, he met John Smith and was so shocked when he died so suddenly the next day. When Tony Blair then came into power, he sent him a mini-mouthorgan. It was so well received they requested he sent a second one, which of course he did. I could never understand why, when they gave parties at No.10 inviting many celebrities from show business, Larry was never invited.

Larry never ever smoked or took drugs and deplored both habits. Special dispensation - I was allowed cigarettes with my coffee.

His overseas wartime tours were mainly with Jack Benny for whom he had a great love and respect. He always told me how he learned so much by way of showmanship from him.

Whenever requested, he gave concerts in Prisons; I was once with him in Wormwood Scrubs. He had composed a piece which he called *Screws Blues*. The prisoners loved it and oh how they loved his shows.

One time there was an exhibition of various items for sale and I bought a key ring with a rather large brass medallion etched with the prison gates and the words HM Prison Wormwood Scrubs. Often when asked my address I proffer the key ring!

Larry appeared as a guest of Michael Parkinson together with Lilly Palmer and Itzhak Perlman. Totally unrehearsed, the two musicians played *Summertime*. So breathtakingly beautiful was the sound they produced that this programme is in the BBC Archives. I treasure the video copy I have.

We had a somewhat open relationship and over the years it was generally assumed we were more than an item - I was usually addressed as Mrs Adler and Larry always whispered to me "let it go". After the Memorial service, outside the theatre was a man I knew so well by sight always waiting on the pavement after a big event, together with the paparazzi, when he came to me and said, "I had to come to pay my respects Mrs Adler". I was very touched and didn't want to disillusion him. I sometimes wished Larry could more easily separate the sincere from the sycophants - he would then have known which path to take.

He often said to me that had his autobiography been of the "bed-hopping" genre it would have sold many more copies. I know in all those years of fame he "hopped" with impunity, so I admired the fact that he spared the blushes of many. Once, in Japan, he knew he was to meet a lady he'd had fun with in the past. He told me with some surprised bewilderment "... but she looked so old". I said, "It was maybe 20 or 30 years since you last met, perhaps she thought you had aged too!"

Larry had a fabulous smile and great charm so that many women, young enough to be his daughter or even granddaughter, were attracted to him and tried to keep in touch even from as far afield as Australia.

I miss that smile and the tactile relationship, which was a great comfort to me in times of stress.

Larry's Quirks and Idiosyncrasies

- Any cliché would bring a look of horror to his face. He could never understand why clichés would constantly impede original thought and expression.

- He had a brilliant but at the same time disorganised mind. He could never be trained to put anything in the same place twice.

- He loved eating biscuits in bed (his bed, not mine!) and on occasions, when I would need to find something in his bedroom, the unmade bed would resemble the gravel path of an airport runway.

- It so happens I make good iced borscht; I could buy him with a plate of my borscht.

- He was a very friendly soul and more inclined to see only good in people - the sycophants - the hyperbole and the Green room ecstasy. He thought I was too critical or analytical of people whereas in fact I simply had a more logical approach.

- When I first knew him he was unaware that a pair of socks were meant to match each other; we soon cured that!

- To queue was anathema to him unless it was a matter of life or death.

- Hated raucous laughter in restaurants - sign of vulgarity, attention seeking and just plain bad manners when we were unable to talk above the noise.

- Loathed the word "tummy" especially when used even by Medics.

- Refused to enter a cinema before main feature as he did not wish to see adverts or trailers.

- He had been a possible subject for *This is Your Life* but found it cloying and embarrassing and said if ever caught he would simply walk off the set, and knowing him as I did, I firmly believe that would have been his reaction.

- At the theatre, if the show was not to his liking, he would walk out pretty damn quick.

- "Keep your fingers crossed" would make him cringe -me too (after all crossed fingers never ever stopped any kind of calamity and certainly no an unwanted pregnancy; a useless contraception!)

I think one disappointment in his last years was not to be proclaimed as *Oldie of the Year* at the annual *Oldie* luncheons at Simpsons. Larry was talking to a very attractive looking man. Not unnaturally I said, "My, he's something of a Lady Killer, who is he?" Larry replied; "Indeed, he's Count Von Bullow!"

Mea Culpa

Of course I wasn't always right, but not so generous of spirit as Larry to admit it. He would listen to my occasional tirade and quietly say, "Of course I agree with all your comments, accusations, criticism or whatever" thereby being exonerated and gently adding, "so come and lie down with me", that in order to put behind us that particular war.

On one of Larry's last overseas engagements, he bought a gift for me. Usually it was perfume or good costume jewellery. This time it was a full size, quite expensive pale blue Pashmina. Now I had for some time been wearing Pashminas when it first became a fashion 'must'. I had several in different colours but the one I had first and wore more than any other was the same pale blue. I could not believe that he was so unaware of having seen it very many times and asked him (after profuse thanks) would he mind terribly if I changed it for another colour. He agreed to give me the receipt in order to effect the exchange. However, deep down, Larry was a very sensitive soul and I can't remember ever seeing him so very obviously hurt and disappointed. He said nothing to make me feel guilty but within an hour said, did I mind if he went home early and left looking so very crestfallen. It was never mentioned again and I had the cream coloured wrap that I wanted, but always I regretted having so needlessly upset him.

The last eighteen months of our life together were greatly marred by a person who had no right to feature in his life at all. In fact, we did not speak at all from February to April 2001.

Our last three months together were, therefore, all the more important and poignant. I feel very honoured to be the first and only person mentioned in his Will outside of course, his brother and four children.

His ear for music was such that he had 'perfect pitch'. This would be evident in that if he had to read lines in a foreign language - one he had never learned - not only the pronunciation but also the cadence would be such that it would be 'sans accent'.

In my opinion he was never filled with his own importance, could never be described as a snob. He was relatively modest and affable.

Despite this genius, I found him somewhat gullible. Often, for me, logic would make me positively doubt what I heard but he accepted without question even from those who were questionable. He was not always quintessentially "Mr Nice Guy" but a quick flash of temper would not usually last very long. The chemistry between us stemmed from probity and mutual rectitude, and for these reasons we always forgave each other. The essence of our relationship was mutual respect and the fact that we could turn anger to laughter in a very short time.

We both hated it when certain words became very popular and were used repeatedly in answer to any question, words such as basically, definitely, and above all hopefully, which was rarely used with grammatical correctness.

Gloria and Larry With kind permission of Peter Golding

Larry liked to play around with the expression 'Phallic feelings' so would, I think, have been amused to know his Memorial Concert took place in the theatre which staged that same night, *The Vagina Monologues*.

‘I have no self-discipline - find it difficult to succumb to the tyranny of the typewriter - I am in fact inordinately lazy.’

What I have written here is not Larry’s life story and it’s not mine. It’s perhaps a series of vignettes of just little incidents; random thoughts that come to my mind about the years we were together that will provide perspective to our relationship.

We had so many highs and lows together; so many memories. In so many ways I shall miss him. His wonderful music, and the great bond that existed between us for all of these years.

He was very much my life and it was a very different kind of life, one where it is impossible to pick up the pieces now that he has gone.

Issey Miyake

"I had the great pleasure of inviting Larry san to Tokyo in 1990 for an exhibition "PLEATS PLEASE". He played his harmonica with the children at the reception party. I was thrilled with the rhythm of his harmonica, which echoed perfectly with the undulation and swell of pleats."

LARRY ADLER by Peter Stringfellow

There is no doubt about it; Larry Adler was an exceptional human being.

I first met him when I turned up for lunch at the famous Mayfair restaurant Langans, and for some reason my date didn't turn up. I was hanging around the bar and I was introduced to Larry by Peter Langan who said "Two lonely hearts together" as Larry's lunch date had not turned up either.

We had lunch together and I was far more impressed with Larry than he was with me. Larry was my mother's pin-up boy. She had photos from his very early days, with his harmonica and his dark Latin eyes and dark wavy brylcreemed hair. There were no mobile phones then and I couldn't wait to get back to my apartment and ring my mother, and to say she was impressed is an understatement. We became firm friends until the day he died.

I have many memories of Larry – he was a true Maestro. His hearing was pitch perfect. I know this because he was critical of every pianist that played at my club Stringfellows!

We had conversations about people like Humphrey Bogart and Ingrid Bergman because he knew them intimately. Surprisingly he did not like Humphrey, which is a shame because Humphrey is one of my all-time favourites. And as for Ingrid Bergman that is a story for another time!

Another thing about Larry, he liked a bottle of good red wine, but it really had to be a good wine, and over the years he drank a good few of them in my club Stringfellows, with my compliments.

Larry with Peter Stringfellow at Stringfellows, London 1983 © Richard Young

I must add that the last memory I have of Larry was during the last week of his life when he complained to me that he had not had a good glass of wine for weeks. I sent over a superb vintage Claret, which I know was left opened at the side of the bed, and minutes before he died he opened his eyes and asked for a drink, which was given to him and that was the last thing that Larry did before he passed away.

Larry's autobiography; *It Ain't Necessarily So* is a fantastic story about a great guy!

From Larry's private collection - with kind permission of Marmoset Adler

Sir Michael Parkinson

Larry Adler was an exhausting man. He never stopped talking and rarely listened. He was an indefatigable, unstoppable source of anecdote and reminiscence yet rarely boring. Any man who inspired Malcolm Arnold to write a concerto for mouthorgan, who knew George Gershwin, Duke Ellington and Louis Armstrong and who played a doubles match at tennis partnering Charlie Chaplin against Greta Garbo and Salvador Dali, must be worth listening to. He came to England because he was blacklisted during the terrible McCarthy Communist witch hunt in America. Their loss, our gain. He was responsible for one of the moments on the show I shall never forget when he improvised a version of *Summertime* with Itzhak Perlman, the poignancy of which will haunt me until the day I die.

From '*Parky's People*' (published by Hodder & Stoughton)

Itzhak Perlman

As a violinist, the best compliment I can pay to Larry Adler is to say that he was the Heifetz of the harmonica: His beautiful tone, energy, musicianship and incredible technique transformed the harmonica into an instrument deserving of the concert stage.

His repertoire was enormous from classical to popular to Jazz and he was comfortable in all.

I had the opportunity to perform on television, a Gershwin selection with him during one of my visits to London. It was a musical experience I shall never forget.

He was a great artist.

Michael Parkinson, Larry Adler & Itzhak Perlman – The Parkinson Show
© Illustration by Michael Italiaander

Larry at 75

Produced by von Saxe Associates

Larry at 80

As Larry approached the age of 80, he felt it was the right time to create a new recording and was considering another in the classical genre. That was until the opportunity to a more 'popular' approach which led to the fabulous album, *The Glory of Gershwin.*

wonderful music memories, I also recounted when having been invited to meet President Clinton at the White House with Charlotte Church, I asked Larry – a man never short of an opinion or an answer - for some thoughts on what I should say.

Jonathan Shalit © Portrait by Italiaander

Like so many whose lives he touched in myriad ways, I will always owe Larry a special debt of gratitude. For all of us, every career has to have a beginning, a point at which uncertain ambition takes form in the green shoots of achievement. My own chosen career path and the success I have enjoyed in it emanates very largely from meeting and taking inspiration from the friendship, generosity and unique talents of Larry Adler.

I owe him my eternal thanks and love.

The Glory of Gershwin recording includes:

Peter Gabriel, Chris De Burgh, Sting, Lisa Stansfield, Sir Elton John, Carly Simon, Elvis Costello, Cher, Kate Bush, Jon Bon Jovi, Oleta Adams, Willard White, Sinéad O'Connor, Robert Palmer, Meat Loaf, Issy Van Randwyck, Courtney Pine and Sir George Martin.

Such was the demand that other celebrity musicians had to be excluded from the recording due to lack of space.

Sir George Martin

I am so pleased to be part of this tribute to Larry whom I remember as an extraordinary musician with a passion for playing music right up to the end of his long life. When I was asked to make a record with him celebrating his 80th birthday, I was amazed at how many young artists clamoured for the chance to play on his record.

Sir George Martin and Larry Adler at Air Studios, Hampstead.
With kind permission of Tatiana von Saxe Wilson

The strongest impression of Larry was his youthful enthusiasm and amazing fund of amusing stories of people he had met during his long and eventful life. It was wonderful to hear of his time as a young man with Hollywood stars such as Ingrid Bergman, Fred Astaire and Clark Gable. Of course Larry was a compulsive name-dropper but he really did know the greatest of people and for me it was wonderful to work with such a legend.

Sting was the first artist to join us on the Gershwin project having already had Larry as a guest on his live concerts, together with Elton John, Elvis Costello, Sinead O'Connor, Carly Simon, Peter Gabriel, Chris de Burgh and many others. Larry was particularly proud of his friendship with George Gershwin and so *The Glory of Gershwin* was born.

Larry was able to bring into play his gift for playing jazz as well as classical music together with an immense sensitivity with his interpretation of Gershwin's glorious songs. The result was wonderful and one of the best records I ever produced.

Cher

My fondest memory of Larry was on the evening of the wrap party for the Gershwin album. We were sitting at the piano together. He started playing the old 40's classics quietly and I started to sing, because I knew all of them.

Larry said, "I haven't had this much fun since Judy (Garland) and I did this." It was probably the greatest compliment anyone has ever paid me!"

Larry with Cher at the recording of *The Glory of Gershwin*
From Larry's private collection - with kind permission of Marmoset Adler

Sting

© Kevin Mazur

I was in a band in Newcastle in the early seventies; we played a lot of covers, some Jazz standards, Soul, Blues and a few originals. One of my favourite covers was a simple Jazz waltz called *Way Down East*, written by Larry

Adler. I loved that tune, but the idea that I would one day meet and work with the composer was simply beyond the bounds of possible, and I never imagined moving in circles where such luminaries would enter my orbit, or me theirs.

A decade later, having reached some level of luminosity myself, I felt confident enough to place a call with Larry's management and ask him to help me out on a song I had just composed. The song was called *Shape of My Heart* and I wanted the sound of a chromatic harmonica to grace its middle section. Why not contact the best in the business; the name synonymous with the mastery of that difficult and demanding instrument, Larry Adler himself.

I was flattered that he'd heard of me and was intrigued enough to come down from London to my house in Wiltshire. We took a walk before lunch in my garden and I outlined my plan for the track, but Larry was distracted by the sight of my tennis court.

"Do you play?" he enquired.

"Well yes!" I replied, “Though not very well."

"Perfect!" said Larry, "Let's play!"

I forget how old Larry was at the time, suffice to say he was considerably older than me (albeit spry), so I thought maybe a few balls over the net between us would be a relaxing entree into the recording session. Two hours later, Larry is two sets up, 6-4, 6-2; drop shots, back hand volleys, ground shots and serving devastating aces with more 'spin' than a state department press briefing. I'm wondering where this man gets his energy from; the third set is simply beyond my ability to salvage. 5-0 down with Larry about to serve for the match.

“Shall we head to the studio now?” he asked.

I dropped my racquet and slumped off the court in abject defeat, relieved not to have been further humiliated by a final coup de grace delivered with searing accuracy and insouciant élan. His energy in the studio was equal to his grace on the court, virtually one take and as close to perfection as one would dare to expect.

"Another game of tennis?” said Larry.

I resolved to take a year of lessons before I took on this wonder again.

"Perhaps next year Larry, my elbow's playing up!"

A year after that Larry had agreed to perform at Carnegie Hall for The Rainforest Foundation’s benefit concert, with a full orchestra, playing Gershwin's *Rhapsody in Blue*. An almost unbelievable feat, except I was there in the wings, open mouthed like the rest of the audience.

I was proud to call him my friend, proud to stand on the same stage as him, and sad that we never got to play tennis again. *Way Down East* is still one of my favourite tunes.

Larry with his *Glory of Gershwin* presentation disc © Italiaander

Andrew McKinnon

© Portrait by Italiaander

Larry first came to Australia in 1938. It was a memorable tour since it provided the opportunity for his honeymoon; for his first encounters with many life-long friends such as Neilma Gantner and other members of the Myer family; and for his first performance with an orchestra.

The Sydney Symphony Orchestra's proposal initially alarmed Larry, who did not read music. However, showing true showbiz daring, he proceeded with the idea of

that least of all Larry. When the night came and the lights went out, and Larry stood in the darkness ready to start, everyone involved thought Oh Shit! What if he can't see anything and stumbles? And maybe a few of the audience as well.

He played, the lights came up, we sighed a small sigh of relief. Now he had to get down those stairs, playing the harmonica. In rehersal he played with two hands, but now he needed one hand to hold the rail as he walked down. How was he going to make this work? Simple. He grabbed the balistrade with one hand - played with the other - and on long sustained notes, strode down that stair as confident and as professional as ever. Another sigh.Then he negotiated an improvised path through the furniture to the piano, just in time for the duet... Whew! I'm sure the audience sighed as well. If nothing else that opening got everyones attention. All the rest was Larry's magic how he seduced the Sexy but vulnerable Issy Van Randwick with harmonica and charm was a joy to behold. Clive Rowe joined them with his tenor voice singing like Gabriel's horn and with a syncopation in phrasing that sparked Larry's talent for making the harmonica swing. This little presentation went from England to Australia.

I will miss that rascal, cause that's what he was. He's probably dropping names of those of us left here on earth to those whose names he dropped to us who had passed on. You know what I mean?

God Bless you Larry
Yours
Clarke P

Larry's Friends

Larry had a large, varied and interesting group of friends that he had met on his travels all over the world. These included many famous celebrity names as well as members of many Royal families.

From Larry's private collection - with kind permission of Marmoset Adler

Baron Marc Burca

Larry, in his twilight years used to be the food editor of 'BOARDROOM' a magazine I founded in 1982. As editor, Larry and I met often both for business and socially. Larry was full stories.

Larry was expelled from the USA during the McCarthy era for being a Hollywood Communist subversive and certainly played harmonica for the Labour Party during the period that Lord Neil Kinnock was leader. However, Larry crossed both sides of the spectrum enjoying the High Life with the Rich and Famous whilst telling restaurants that he was going to review them, thereby eating "gratis". Despite having a reputation in the restaurant community for this his reviews were still objective and written a "Larry chatty way". I still have all his reviews.

Larry loved jokes... he especially loved telling Jewish jokes. Even if the jokes were not always very funny, in Larry's hands they were always funny. He had the art of the comedian - "It's the way I tell them".

Larry and I often met for lunch or dinner and we always had an amusing time. He would never talk politics but normally talk about his days in the USA with George Gershwin, his daily tennis with Charlie Chaplin in the 40's or with Victor Lowndes (the head of the Playboy Club in Park Lane) in the 1980's and that he had been secretly engaged to Ingrid Bergman. His favourite story was the "Marc I have the best social climbing story in history to tell you" (his tennis story with Charlie Chaplin).

But if ever the conversation was lacking a good way of stoking it up was to mention Tatiana Von Saxe who he could talk about for hours as being the "love of his life". He was forever proposing marriage to Tatiana and hung out at her very popular restaurant 'Café Delancey'. I spent New Year with them both there once. I also took Andrew Neil the then editor of the Sunday Times and Kristian Becker the German TV presenter on MTV there after we had spent time at the MTV studios.

The BBC did a documentary about Larry and I went with him to view it at Tatiana's place in North London. Tatiana was happily married at the time to Mr Wilson, however Larry constantly came out with "I WANT TO MARRY YOUR WIFE" she is the love of my life.... Although he meant it, he said it in such an amusing way that it always seemed forgivable!

Larry was very approachable and although a bit of a snob on some issues, he could be very open on others especially with music.

On one occasion he came to my house and "jammed" with the beautiful ex-Cheltenham Ladies College nanny Rebeka Byram Wigfield who was 'resting' at the time. She on the piano/singing and he on the harmonica - I taped it and have it somewhere on VHS tape. She was a singer/songwriter who had played at the Casino in Lisbon and who went to further success in New York in the 90's. Larry just joined in and there was an immediate music chemistry.

Sometimes Larry would invite me to the Jazz Club underneath Pizza Express on the Park. Owned by our mutual friend Peter Boizot, the founder of the Pizza Express chain of restaurants. Larry would hold Jazz evenings there sometimes with an old Pianola which had a recording of George Gershwin actually playing (with all the keys moving). The "piece de resistance" was always the "Gershwin/Adler" version of *SUMMERTIME*. He just captured the mood. It was as if GERSHWIN had written the piece for Larry, so good was their synergy.

Tatiana von Saxe Wilson

I met Larry Adler when he came to review *The Café Delancey* as a food critic. His review finished with the sentence: "Tatiana, will you marry me?" People were coming to the Café just to see who this person was and generated great publicity for the restaurant.

Illustration by Larry Adler
From the private collection of Tatiana von Saxe Wilson

That was the beginning of a beautiful friendship lasting from late 1985 to his death. Larry was unique, understanding, caring, gifted, loving, and fun. His wit and ad lib humour inimitable. He felt, when in company his duty was to entertain and so jokes and anecdotes flowed. In private he was reserved, intelligent and always funny. I never saw him angry.

Larry with Tatiana ©Jimmy Moore
From Larry's private collection - with kind permission of Marmoset Adler

The *Café Delancey* 'concept' (free newspapers, any dish available at any time of the day – from 8 am to midnight - no minimum charge, no cover charge and changing atmosphere) took off. Its bar '*Martini's* created '*Larry's* Wallbanger' in his honour.

Larry introduced me to showbiz. I learned how to become a restaurant critic, producer and publisher.

We went out every night to shows, parties and dinners. Larry would draw sketches and cartoons on paper tablecloths or waiters' pads.

© Picture by David Wilson
With kind permission of Tatiana von Saxe Wilson

This I turned into a book *'Have I Ever Told You...'* a compilation of humorous anecdotes and vignettes.

© Delancey Press

Often misunderstood, the public either liked or disliked him but everybody respected and admired him for his musical talent. True to his convictions, Larry did not expect approval or agreement. He often reminded himself to be grateful that he made a living by doing what he loved best - a luxury not many people have. And even better when it is the size of a mouthorgan and easily carried around.

People always recognised his voice which on more than one occasion helped him diffuse what could have been unpleasant situations: Larry's car hit a lorry and when the fuming driver approached him, Larry told him: "I bet you anything that you will use the F word on your first sentence!" They both laughed. Driving against the traffic on a one way street after a show and admitting to the policeman he was aware of what he was doing the policeman asked: "Why did you do it then?" To which Larry replied: "On the off chance of not meeting you...!"

Larry invited his daughter Marmoset and me to accompany him on the maiden voyage of the QE2. On meeting the Queen Mother, she asked to see Larry's mouthorgan and playfully said: "Nobody will believe me when I say I have held Larry's organ in my hand".

Larry had been on the maiden voyage of the QE1 when he was asked to play *Rhapsody in Blue* on air for a first transatlantic transmission but the connection did not work. When told of this at the end of his rendition, Larry asked why had he had not been told before but the crew replied: But WE love *Rhapsody in Blue* and WE wanted to hear it!

With kind permission of Tatiana von Saxe Wilson

At HM Prison *Wormwood Scrubs* Christmas show, Larry just stood on the stage waiting for the conversation to subside. When everybody was finally quiet he announced: "Now that I have a *captive* audience" and started playing

Begin the Beguine to an uproar of applause from the inmates! An amazing evening.

Larry Adler was a widely revered musician, composer, prolific columnist, assiduous world traveller, war correspondent, writer and raconteur. He excelled at all. His talent won him recognition and fame thus raising the mouthorgan to an orchestral instrument. This is his legacy for the benefit of many to follow.

I applaud the author of this book to preserve Larry's memory in the centennial anniversary of Adler's birth.

Illustration by Larry Adler
With kind permission of Tatiana von Saxe Wilson

Lady Olga Maitland

I first met Larry Adler in the 70's through the newspaper world.

The other day, looking through a jewellery case, I found a miniature harmonica with Larry's name inscribed on it. I do treasure this. Larry would always have a handful of harmonicas in his pocket to give to people – and would then demonstrate that he could still play a tune on them, despite them being so small.

Larry was a good friend to everyone – me no exception. In Fleet Street we loved our times having lunch or dinner with him. He was always full of stories – be they Jewish ones or showbiz. In fact his catchword was "Have I ever told you...." which made the title of a book compiling the best. I did laugh at the story;

> An old Jew is dying. His wife sits by his bedside and there is a terrible storm outside. A huge streak of lightening followed by a terrific clap of thunder.
>
> The old man sits up and says: "I'm about to die. Send for a priest.'
>
> "Sam!" His wife says. "You're losing your mind. Surely you mean a rabbi?"
>
> "A rabbi should not go out on a night like this!"

Lady Olga Maitland – from her private collection

Larry was fun. His humour was prodigious. I recall one time when we had a party at our home. It was Christmas. We had a small choir singing carols. We served a hot ham dish. Larry laughed and said, “That is a hell of a party to serve up to a good Jewish boy!” He then topped it all, and played the harmonica for us.

He was full of surprises too. One day he called me up. He needed, at short notice, somewhere to live for a couple of weeks. “No problem,” I said, “come to our home. We always have a bed for you." Well, he arrived accompanied by his long-standing friend Lady Selina Hastings. She left him to our care. He stayed with us for six months.......!

I remember long chats with Larry about his life, his successes and failures. He admitted his biggest failure was procrastination – be it in decision managing about his personal life, his professional life or even getting down to writing his own autobiography. Finally, in desperation, I said that I would interview him on tape, and we would get his story down on paper. We sat for hours in our drawing room – I still have the transcripts. What really came across was that despite being hounded out of the USA, he never bore anybody any bitterness or bad feeling. He seemed to roll with the punches.

In the end he did write his own book – but personally I felt that the story he told me was more vivid.

Away from the stage, his love was tennis. He was a natural. I played with him occasionally but he was always a far better and more stylish player.

On stage, he was magic; Larry's fingers were in constant movement. Flexing them, stretching them – almost playing with the air. I will never forget a concert he gave at the Royal Festival Hall. He played all our old favourites from Genevieve to Gershwin and much else. It was sheer delight.

The great and good came. Larry had friends from all sides of the political divide, be they Labour or Conservative. On this occasion he invited to the Royal Box Neil Kinnock and his wife, Glenys. I regret to say that it was like a red rag to a bull when Neil Kinnock saw me. Politically, in those days we were bitterly opposed, at least on his part. He did everything he could to avoid speaking to me. Tight lipped silence reigned. My husband Robin scaled the heights of conversational skills but to no avail. Finally, through gritted teeth, he said, "I can never bring myself to speak to people like her!" For all that I just laughed. Larry was amused too.

Musically we always enjoyed Larry, but I do slightly wonder why he didn't composed more music during his career, or indeed widen his repertoire. It was always the old favourites which we loved but I felt there was more to be done. Essentially, it was that old devil procrastination creeping in. I wish he had. He was a man of immense and memorable talent.

I miss his fun, his humanity and his very real friendship. This I guess, speaks for us all.

Larry performing with Lord Louis Mountbatten
From Larry's private collection – with kind permission of Marmoset Adler

Larry with Joanna Lumley
From Larry's private collection – with kind permission of Marmoset Adler

Larry with HRH The Princess Royal
From Larry's private collection – with kind permission of Marmoset Adler

Images of Larry

There were a number of occasions to get together with Larry to create images – sometimes suggested by me and at other times by him.

One of the most special was something quite unique …

'Duet'

I consider myself extremely fortunate that I come from an artistic background. It has shaped who I am and everything I do revolves around creative thinking. My father is a superb artist, working mainly in oils; he spent many years as the creative director of a variety of well-known advertising agencies.

I suggested to him, (around 1990 when I had been working for some years as a photographer) that mixing an original photographic portrait with an oil painting would be extremely interesting. This was the era before digital manipulation and it sparked some heated debates. Eventually, we developed a valid reason that made us feel that the combination would really work and we then produced some samples combining the two art forms.

My feeling was simply that a fine photographic portrait would capture the essence of the person in a very different way to the artist's interpretation in paint. It would have been interesting, had the photographic process been around much earlier (having only been invented in the mid 1800's) to record many great historic figures using the photographic process.

As the process combines two different art forms, we decided to call the combination, 'Duet'. However, as it is also a collaboration with the sitter, it provides an alternative reason for the name. It certainly makes an extremely fascinating piece of art when completed.

When I suggested to Larry that he be part of such a collaboration he was extremely interested in the unusual process and keen to do so.

It was vital to know and agree the concept before commencing - which included discussions followed by rough sketches - otherwise the initial photographic portrait might not fit as intended. The photograph created would then be placed onto a specific, pre-determined area of a fine-art canvas so that the oil painting process could then begin.

In Larry's case, he wanted to include a scene from *Porgy and Bess* having been so closely associated with his friends, George and Ira Gershwin. The other element to be included (and which created further debate as to how it might be fitted in) was tennis, which was his passion. The final element was the butterfly – signifying summer and the fluttering of Larry's hands when performing.

The finished portrait can be seen here. Larry was delighted and satisfied that we had achieved what he had in mind.

So I feel it fair, and I feel honoured, to say that I was involved in a 'Duet' with Larry Adler.

Larry's completed 'Duet' © Italiaander

Photographic portraits of Larry by Italiaander

The following, previously unpublished images I took in my studio when unusually, Larry appeared in a suit.

© Italiaander

© Italiaander

© Italiaander

© Italiaander

© Italiaander

© Italiaander

© Italiaander

© Italiaander

© Italiaander

© Italiaander

© Italiaander

© Italiaander

© Italiaander

For the following portraits, I visited Larry at his flat which was very much his place of work. The images show him playing the mouthorgan and piano as well using his computer for his writing.

The portraits here were created in an extremely relaxed atmosphere.

© Italiaander

© Italiaander

© Italiaander

© Italiaander

© Italiaander

© Italiaander

© Italiaander

© Italiaander

© Italiaander

© Italiaander

© Italiaander

© Italiaander

© Italiaander

Larry at 85

To celebrate his 85th birthday, a concert took place at The Queen Elizabeth Hall on Friday 12th February 1999 which included his protégé Antonio Serrano Dalmas and Sir George Martin for a Beatles number. Larry told me he considered this one of the highlights of his life.

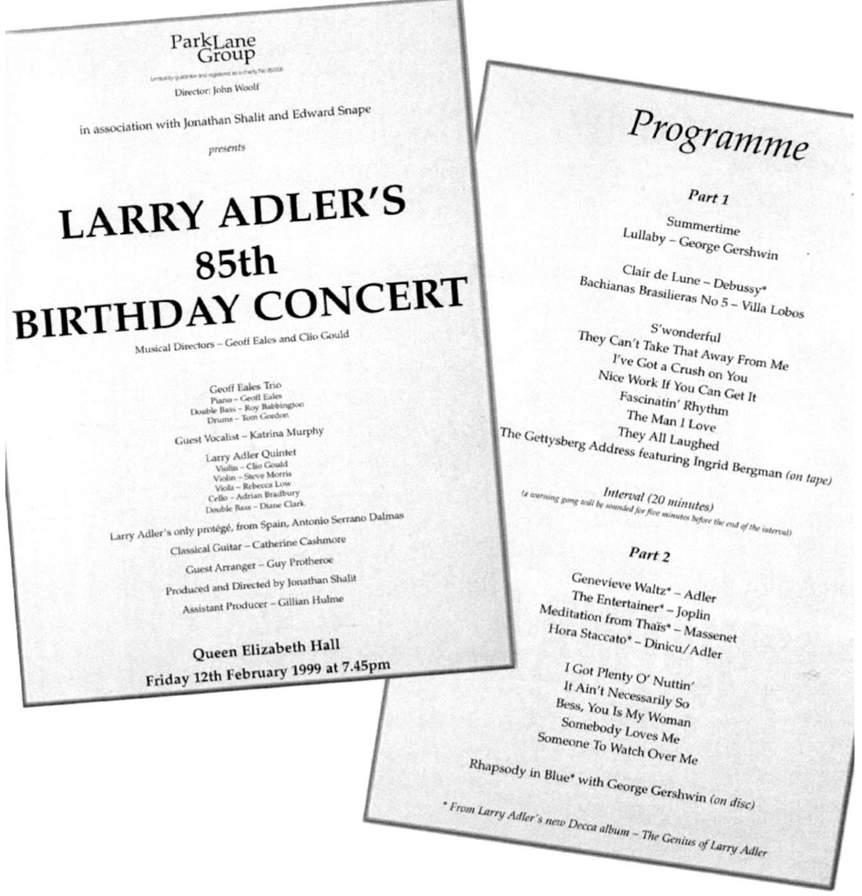

ParkLane Group

Limited by guarantee and registered as a charity No [illegible]

Director: John Woolf

in association with Jonathan Shalit and Edward Snape

presents

LARRY ADLER'S
85th
BIRTHDAY CONCERT

Musical Directors – Geoff Eales and Clio Gould

Geoff Eales Trio
Piano – Geoff Eales
Double Bass – Roy Babbington
Drums – Tom Gordon

Guest Vocalist – Katrina Murphy

Larry Adler Quintet
Violin – Clio Gould
Violin – Steve Morris
Viola – Rebecca Low
Cello – Adrian Bradbury
Double Bass – Diane Clark

Larry Adler's only protégé, from Spain, Antonio Serrano Dalmas

Classical Guitar – Catherine Cashmore

Guest Arranger – Guy Protheroe

Produced and Directed by Jonathan Shalit

Assistant Producer – Gillian Hulme

Queen Elizabeth Hall
Friday 12th February 1999 at 7.45pm

Programme

Part 1

Summertime
Lullaby – George Gershwin

Clair de Lune – Debussy*
Bachianas Brasilieras No 5 – Villa Lobos

S'wonderful
They Can't Take That Away From Me
I've Got a Crush on You
Nice Work If You Can Get It
Fascinatin' Rhythm
The Man I Love
They All Laughed
The Gettysberg Address featuring Ingrid Bergman *(on tape)*

Interval (20 minutes)
(a warning gong will be sounded for five minutes before the end of the interval)

Part 2

Genevieve Waltz* – Adler
The Entertainer* – Joplin
Meditation from Thaïs* – Massenet
Hora Staccato* – Dinicu/Adler

I Got Plenty O' Nuttin'
It Ain't Necessarily So
Bess, You Is My Woman
Somebody Loves Me
Someone To Watch Over Me

Rhapsody in Blue* with George Gershwin *(on disc)*

** From Larry Adler's new Decca album – The Genius of Larry Adler*

Larry performing *Summertime* on mouthorgan and piano
© Italiaander

Larry in concert © Italiaander

Antonio Serrano, harmonica virtuoso - Larry's only protégé.

(Originally written for the 10th anniversary of Larry's death, for Harmonica World - Aug/Sept 2011).

I was only thirteen years old when I first met Larry Adler. It was during the first World Harmonica Championships, in Jersey in 1987, where I was participating together with my family.

After one of my performances as a chromatic harmonica soloist, a middle aged Latin American woman came up to my father and me, and, after introducing herself as Larry Adler's fiancé, she told us that Larry had been very impressed by my ability, being so young, and that he would like to invite me to play with him at a concert in Paris.

Immediately my father said that it was a great idea and that I would be honoured to play with Larry. At the time I didn't really know who Larry Adler was, but watching my father's reaction, I could tell that something serious was going on. We went to have lunch with Larry and after a while he had already figured out that I didn't have a clue about who I was having lunch with. Far from getting upset, he was very kind to me and gave me a cassette tape of him playing works for harmonica and orchestra that I still keep like a treasure.

Back home I listened to the tape again and again and understood that Larry was THE BOSS! It was the first time I heard a harmonica sounding so big and soulful. By listening to Larry I learned that music was much more than hitting the right note at the right time. Having played and shared time with Larry Adler has inspired me through my career till now and when I've had to make difficult decisions in my life I have always spent some time thinking, what would Larry Adler have done in this situation?

Later in my life I was lucky to meet Toots Thielemans and had the opportunity of jamming with him at the Terrasa Jazz Festival and only God knows if someday I will meet Stevie Wonder.

Larry performing with Antonio Serrano © Italiaander

These are for me the three main pillars of the chromatic harmonica. What I have learned from these masters is that honesty, hard work, some talent and a great amount of love are the perfect mix to become a great musician.

Looking back, I realise how fortunate I was to meet Larry Adler when I was only a kid. Maybe music is basically about being at the right place in the right time...

The Hope Charity

After I had known Larry for some time, I asked him whether he would like to be my guest at a charity ball being held at the Dorchester hotel, where we had first met.

The evening was for an organisation that I had been involved with for a number of years called ‘Hope’, a charity set up for children with learning disabilities. Hope had come about when a few families with children that had effectively been given up on by the medical establishment here in the UK, had needed to find an answer elsewhere. They had discovered Professor Reuven Feuerstein whose Institute is based in Israel. He had begun developing his theories in the late 1940's while working with children who had been separated from their parents by the holocaust. The basic principle of the Feuerstein Method is that all human beings - regardless of their age, disability or socio-economic background - have the ability to significantly improve their learning and therefore their level of functioning. The application of the Feuerstein Method leads to the enhancement of peoples' learning potential, improvement of their cognitive functioning, and enables them to learn how to learn.

My first association with Hope came about when I was asked by a friend, Gina Drew-Davis who was Hope’s administrator, if I could help by taking some photographs of the children for the brochure that was being prepared for the annual ball. These events were always significant as the charity existed mostly on donations. I was aware that this was for a very good cause and I had always made a point of offering my services where possible for the benefit of children. Before long, I had become a member of the fund-raising team providing all the creative requirements for Hope. And, as my gallery was in Harrods at the time, with my connections, I was also able to include Harrods in contributing some gifts to our raffle.

When I invited Larry, it was purely as a guest without any request or expectation that he might do anything specific - I would never have been so presumptuous to do so! On the Friday evening, the day before the ball, he phoned me to tell me he had fallen onto a radiator in his flat and gashed his arm badly and therefore was unlikely to be able to come. I said that I was sorry to hear that, hoped he was ok and wished him a speedy recovery.

Imagine my complete surprise therefore, when my wife Tamar and I arrived at the Dorchester Hotel the next night, to discover that Larry was indeed there, early, with his partner Gloria Leighton. He looked terrible with his arm heavily bandaged. Everyone was concerned, as by this time he was quite frail and probably should have been resting at home, but that most certainly wasn't Larry's way of doing things. In his mind, he'd been invited and therefore he had to be there.

I then recalled an incident he told me about when, already in his eighties, he had fallen off a stage backwards during a concert rehearsal. Once the doctors had checked him over in hospital, he insisted that he returned to the stage for the evening's performance. He said that he hadn't realised just how close the edge of the stage was and had therefore remained in a relaxed, rather than rigid, state as he fell to the ground. Fortunately he was uninjured and just shocked by the incident.

During the Hope evening, members of the committee said to me, 'please tell Larry to enjoy the evening but we do not ask or expect anything of him'. Larry, on hearing this was almost outraged! His view was that he had come along and intended to perform for the benefit of the charity. It had never even occurred to me that he might do so, let alone in the poor state he was in.

At the appropriate time, Larry insisted that he play for the audience and made his way onto the dance floor where a chair was then placed for him to sit on (which he needed). He made it quite clear that he only ever performed from the stage and then proceeded, with some assistance, onto the stage area. He took out his mouthorgan and played, producing a quality of sound that was so beautiful, the room was absolutely silent with many reduced to tears. At the end of the performance, he and Professor Feuerstein warmly embraced.

We raised huge financial support for Hope that night - so essential for the charity to be able to provide its services - and there is no question that the amount raised was enhanced by Larry's incredibly moving performance.

Opening of the Hope Centre

When I told Larry about the forthcoming opening of the Hope Centre which was to take place on 27th March 2001, once again he was there accompanied by Gloria.

It had taken a number of years to develop the centre and was based on the methodology used by the Feuerstein Institute in Jerusalem. We were delighted that he was able to share the occasion with us, sadly one of his last appearances in public. As always, he played on that occasion as well. A number of other celebrity friends of Hope, also joined us for this very special occasion: Susan Hampshire, Maureen Lipman, Uri Geller, Sidney Corob (Hope's Life President) with his wife Elizabeth, and of course Professor Reuven Feuerstein accompanied by his son Professor Rafi Feuerstein.

Professor Reuven Feuerstein with Larry Adler

L – R: Susan Hampshire, Larry Adler, Maureen Lipman, Uri Geller, Professor Reuven Feuerstein, Professor Rafi Feuerstein, Sidney and Elizabeth Corob

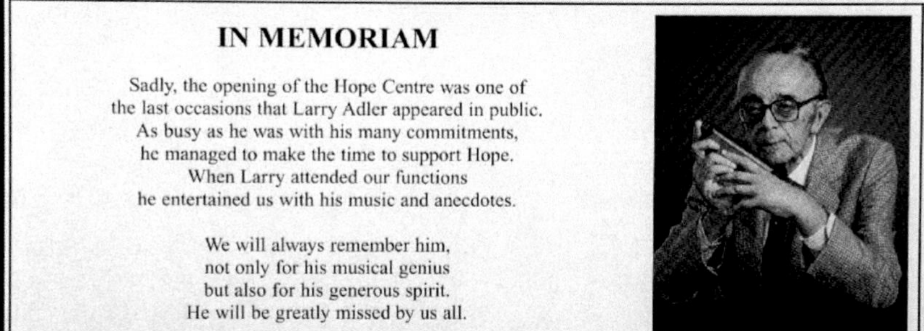

IN MEMORIAM

Sadly, the opening of the Hope Centre was one of
the last occasions that Larry Adler appeared in public.
As busy as he was with his many commitments,
he managed to make the time to support Hope.
When Larry attended our functions
he entertained us with his music and anecdotes.

We will always remember him,
not only for his musical genius
but also for his generous spirit.
He will be greatly missed by us all.

The insert that appeared in the 2002 Hope brochure following Larry's death

Professor Reuven Feuerstein, the world-renowned cognitive psychologist known for his ground-breaking research in cognitive modifiability and founder and director of the Feuerstein Institute in Jerusalem.

Professor Reuven Feuerstein © Portrait by Italiaander

Professor Reuven Feuerstein

To the family of the most beloved Harmonica player and awe inspiring human being, Larry Adler, **זכר צדיק לברכה**.

Without any hesitation, I attribute the concept of "righteous" as a source of blessing to Larry Adler. His wonderful way of making human beings vibrate with music was, and still is, a blessing to those who had the great joy to hear him.

Dear friends, I am sure you remember my last meeting with Larry, on the Inauguration of the new Hope Centre, when he played in my honour a few parts of *Jerusalem of Gold*. By the end, when I came to him, he hugged me and kissed me and offered the Harmonica to me: "take it, take it he insisted, it's yours, I want you to take it". I stepped back and told him, I cannot take it from your golden mouth.

I don't know if he felt rejected or if he felt the respect I have to him and this wonderful instrument. I am telling you this because I don't know if I was right to reject his generous and most wonderful offer or if I was wrong.

I would like you to know that he will always be in our heart and the air will continue to vibrate his music for eternity.

As it was said by our sages, there is a sound which has been emitted at the Genesis which continues to travel from one corner of the world to the other. Is this not his music?

David and Gillian Helfgott

We first met Larry Adler in the mid-eighties at a private party of a friend of David's professor at the time, Peter Feutchwanger.

It was a delightful affair in a private home in London and Larry wandered over to the piano where David was playing and very soon he and David were performing *Rhapsody in Blue*. It was one of those incredibly special moments in life when you know you are witnessing something truly unique. They both obviously loved Gershwin and the atmosphere they created was something the composer would have relished.

Larry with Simon Tedeschi (L) and David Helfgott (R)
With kind permission of David & Gillian Helfgott

We again had the good fortune to meet Larry when he was performing at the City Recital Centre in Angel Place with Simon Tedeschi accompanying him and what a memorable recital they gave. Again the heart of Gershwin was with us. We also shared lunch with Larry and Simon at the Hilton Hotel in Sydney. Larry was such a brilliant raconteur and the lunch was full of fun and wit and one of the few times David stayed at a luncheon table for the whole meal!

Also, Larry's book *It Ain't Necessarily So* is a must read.

What a great musician and entertainer. The world is richer for his presence.

Issy van Randwyck

I first met Larry in the summer of 1991. I had worked with his son, Peter, in Krakow in the spring of that year and when Larry said that he wanted to take a show to the Ricky DeMarco Gallery in Edinburgh for the Festival and needed a singer, Peter very kindly suggested me.

My audition was a meeting at Larry's flat in Hampstead where we played through *Night and Day* and *Every Time We Say Goodbye* with Larry, one hand on the piano and the other holding the harmonica whilst accompanying. And so a great musical love affair started. I felt like a fish swimming in a perfectly synchronised shoal. We had a great success up at the Festival and continued working until he became sick in 2001.

On returning from Edinburgh, I was doing a solo show at the Pizza on the Park in London and Larry was kindly 'guesting' for me when a friend of mine, Jonathan Shalit came to see the show one night and asked me about Larry. He knew nothing about him and kindly drove Larry home after the show. At 1am my phone rang with Jonathan in a twitter of excitement – "You never told me he was a genius – he's worked with everyone!" I said I knew that. "Well he's going to be 80 next year, something has to be done about it" Well, I said to him, there is your project and off indeed he went and got the album *The Glory of Gershwin* off the ground which George Martin produced and featured a host of music stars of the moment. It also opened another chapter in Larry's life. The album was a hit around the world and I was lucky enough to be able to tour with him and the album to Europe, Barbados, New Zealand, Australia and all around the UK.

I remember so vividly one of the last concerts we did up at Hunstanton in Norfolk. He was very frail and a bed had been put in the wings allowing him to rest until the moment he had to come on stage. Anyone who saw him lying there could never believe that he could possibly do a show let alone hold an audience in the palm of his hand. The physical transformation from Larry in repose to Larry in front of an audience was palpable. He was utterly brilliant and the energy from performing in front of an audience seemed to revitalize his being. He never failed to give his all, no matter how unwell he was feeling, he never failed to make the audience laugh – his comic timing was second to none.

I miss him and his genius to this day.

Larry with Issy van Randwyck © Adrian Houston

Penny Ephson-Clarke

My husband, Clarke Peters, had worked with Larry, staging and directing a presentation of *The Glory of Gershwin* and a couple of years after our son, Max, was born, Larry's manager (Jonathan Shalit) offered me part time work as Larry's personal assistant. It was 1998 and Larry was 84. I had of course met him before and been enthralled by his performances and I remembered my grandmother and my father talking about the great Larry Adler. It seemed surreal that he was to become part of my life. I did not know what to expect but as soon as I entered Larry's flat I knew I had a challenge on my hands!

Larry lived in genteel poverty in a small flat in which there was not a surface (table, chair or floor) that wasn't covered by piles of paper... letters, music sheets, cassettes, decades of New Yorker and Oldie magazines... moth-eaten clothes spilled out of cupboards and drawers, all of which Larry seemed perfectly happy to live with. However, his management needed him to dress more smartly for his public appearances and his flat to be more presentable to visitors. Also, because he had had so many car accidents (fortunately minor) and parking fines it was hoped that I could persuade him to stop driving. How on earth was I going to tactfully achieve any of this?

Hoping he wouldn't notice, I would remove unwearable clothes and Gloria, his partner, would discreetly replace them with new ones. I rarely saw him in any. Larry loved his black Issy Miyake jacket with the red cuffs but apart from that, clothes held little interest for him.

We hadn't quite got round to buying new shoes when Larry returned one day and glared at me saying that he had written off his car and that it was all my fault. He had driven off that morning in his beloved red Alpha Romeo sports car and into the back of a bus. And I was to blame because he had no idea where I had put his shoes and the only ones he could find were a pair of tennis sneakers that were two sizes too big.

Larry was icy for days. No stories, no quips. However, it was worth it. I could tick 'no driving' off my list. But not for long.

A few days later I pulled up at a main road in Maida Vale and turning into the same road from the other side was a car that appeared to have no driver. Then I noticed familiar horned rimmed glasses just visible above the steering wheel. Larry was driving again. I was worried... what did he have on his feet? So, nervously I followed him, until eventually he got home safely. Eventually, because he drove no faster than 10 miles an hour.

The parking tickets and body work repair bills continued.

As time went on, Larry would phone me at home: "Penny, where are my glasses?" and I would suggest places where they might be. Invariably I'd have to drive over to find them, usually with Max in tow. Whilst I was searching, Larry would patiently entertain Max who was totally transfixed, watching him play his mouthorgan. Max loved going to see Larry and called him 'my other grandfather'. Gloria was 'Auntie Larry'.

I too was transfixed whenever Larry played. Sitting at his hall table sorting through requests from autograph seekers and charities, I would listen to Larry practise and sometimes make a request for my favourite *Summertime* or *Rhapsody in Blue*. When I think of those moments I get goose bumps.

What a privilege! Thank you Larry for playing. Just for me. And Larry, you were, as always, right. It was of no consequence whatsoever that you were wearing your dressing gown... and tennis shoes.

Miss you Larry and hope that you are re-united with your red Alpha Romeo Spider.

Simon Tedeschi

The first time I met Larry was in the University of New South Wales in Sydney, where we were to rehearse as part of his first performance in his 2000 Australian tour. I walked into the studio, and was immediately taken aback by the man's diminutive stature – it had not occurred to me that in the 5 years since I had seen the man perform on television, age would have taken its toll. He was wearing his customary 'Issy Miyake' suit, which draped on the wonderful man like gleaming pyjamas. I tried not to catch his eye – I was in the prescence of a great man - and I realised in the front of my mind that playing Gershwin for Adler was akin to playing Beethoven for Beethoven.

I sat down, and we played. It was a magical rush, because we gelled instantly. Adler put down his mouthorgan, and chuckled at me in Baltimore brogue. 'Kid, you're pretty good. I won't criticize you yet, because I don't wanna embarrass you in front of everybody.' Fantastic. Just fantastic. Little did I know that Larry was also in shell-shock from our performance.

Over the next year and a half, Larry and I became like father and son. We ate together, argued, played music together, and loved each other. I think it is safe to say that I saw the private side of Larry – the genius riddled with self-doubt, painfully aware of his impending mortality (whilst denying any possible existence of an afterlife, of course).

We played in Switzerland, Italy, Barbados, England, Scotland and France, and every performance was different. Travelling with him was an experience in itself, hardly suitable for this publication. Tidal waves on Larry's cruise-ship balcony, motion sickness on board the Orient Express,

Simon Tedeschi © Portrait by Italiaander

and the throng of admirers besieging him after one of our many performances in Pizza on the Park in London.

I could easily talk further about Larry's personal help, his humour, his performances, his frustration with his own decelerating body, his infuriating gullibility, his moral support and his jokes (NOT riddles- remember – 'omit needless words.' That was the maxim that Larry lived by.). But instead, I will leave you with something Larry said to me, shortly before his passing.

'Son, (that's what he called me), you're not my accompanist. We're two soloists.'

I will always miss him.

LARRY'S FINAL CURTAIN CALL

'Thank you Larry' by Roger Trobridge.

Past Chairman of the NHL (National Harmonica League), Editor of 'Harmonica World'.

After Larry Adler's death in 2001 there was a memorial concert in The Arts Theatre in London. It was a time to remember him. His family and friends from the musical and literary world were there to reminisce and perform music in his honour.

I was Chairman of the UK harmonica community, the NHL, and Larry was our President, so I talked about what Larry had done for our members and the whole world of the harmonica. He inspired a generation of players. But how did he do it?

In the first two decades of the 1900s, tremolo and diatonic harmonicas had featured in local concerts, contests and on the musical hall stage. Some national figures had emerged, but they remained local, as communications were relatively poor.

Larry was born in 1914 in Baltimore, and soon showed his musical talent and precociousness. He was fortunate to take up the harmonica at the same time as Hohner began to manufacture their new chromatic harmonica; it allowed

Larry Adler: brilliant musician, formidable campaigner by Richard Ingrams

I was among friends and family who packed a chapel at Golders Green Crematorium, to hear more than two hours of tributes to Larry Adler. In accordance with Larry's wishes – he was an inveterate atheist who refused to recognise the supernatural in any shape or form – there were no religious observances.

Most speakers remembered Larry the musician – the man who made the mouthorgan respectable and for whom composers like Vaughan Williams, Darius Millhaud and Malcolm Arnold wrote original pieces – the man who when he was over 80 made the hit parade with a George Gershwin CD accompanying singers like Sinead O'Connor and Elton John.

But Larry was more than just a brilliant musician. He was a campaigner – one of the few Hollywood stars who refused to collaborate in any way with Senator Joseph McCarthy's 1950's witch-hunt, so ending up being blackballed by the American film industry. He was also one of a small band of artists who was prepared to demonstrate his support for Salmon Rushdie by taking part in a public reading of the Satanic Verses – at the time a very courageous thing to do.

The Larry I knew best was the compulsive writer of letters to the press, especially to 'Private Eye'. How this began I cannot now recall. It may have had something to do with Auberon Waugh accusing him of stealing a bag of toffees from Fortnum & Mason. From that point there was scarcely an issue of the 'Eye' which didn't include an Adler letter. He had the distinction of being featured in two of the magazine's Look-a-likes – one with Desmond Tutu, the other with ET.

Ian Hislop never shared my admiration for Larry's humour. So when I launched the 'Oldie' in 1992 I engaged Larry to review old videos which he continued to do until shortly before his death. The success of the column was partly due to the fact that there was hardly a single Hollywood star whom Larry had not known and about whom he could not tell some pointed, if occasionally disrespectful, anecdote.

Larry sitting in 'Genvieve' – the car from the film
From Larry's private collection – with kind permission of Marmoset Adler

Of course he was a name-dropper (someone even suggested that he should have titled his memoirs 'Name Drops Keep Falling On My Head') but no one had a better right to drop names. Had he not, after all, been engaged to Ingrid Bergman and played tennis with Charlie Chaplin, Salvador Dali and Greta Garbo? Only in the presence of Rachmaninov, he admitted, had he been tongue-tied.

Larry writing the score for *A High Wind in Jamaica*
From Larry's private collection – with kind permission of Marmoset Adler

But Larry was much more than just a glorified hobnobber with celebrities. As his video reviews revealed, he was a man of taste, a sensitive and discerning critic with an unerring eye for false sentimentality or humbug. As the man who had composed the music for *Genevieve* and *A High Wind In Jamaica*, he was always (unlike most critics) aware of the vital importance of a film score. Wasn't it the zither music that made *The Third Man* so memorable?

I often said that Larry's *Oldie* column was my personal favourite and I thing he was surprised and flattered. At any rate, he once wrote to me: "It's very kind of you to throw me the occasional bone of approval for my film reviews. At such moments I think of you as the nicest, cutest, most adorable little editor in the whole wide world".

It is the nicest compliment that anyone ever paid me.

(From an article published in The Guardian Newspaper, 12 August 2001)

Larry Adler

PAUL TAYLOR *remembers the maestro of the harmonica – and blagging*

'We've just been asked to do Larry Adler,' my wife, Suzie, the well-known Australian publicist, announced, putting down the phone.

'Who's Larry Adler?' chorused Christine and Kendra.

'Larry Adler knew Ingrid Bergman and Greta Garbo,' I explained. 'Possibly intimately. He played doubles tennis with Dali and Paulette Goddard and Charlie Chaplin. Possibly in the nude. He knew all these people. Al Capone, the Duke and Duchess of Windsor, Cary Grant. Everyone. He's just recorded something with Sting and Elvis Costello. He's a friend of the Duke of Edinburgh. He talks about them all in his *Oldie* column. He's the undisputed heavyweight-champion name-dropper, he's – '

'Good,' said Suzie. 'He's coming to Melbourne. You can meet him at the airport and look after him.'

I waited for Larry to fly in from Tasmania. The dozen or so passengers on the light plane filed out through Gate 29. Not one looked remotely like Larry, an octogenarian whose googly eyes I was familiar with courtesy of *The Oldie*.

I phoned Suzie. 'He's not on it.'

'Nonsense. Go to the luggage carousel.'

I went to the carousel. Round and round it trundled until the last luggage had been picked up and I was left standing alone with the sinking feeling that somehow I had lost someone I'd never met. Then, from behind the plastic strip curtain, an attractive young girl emerged, pushing a wheelchair in which a little eighty-year-old man sat clutching his luggage. He had googly eyes. Larry Adler! In a wheelchair! Oh, Lordie I'd have to get him and his chair in and out of the car wherever we went. At the top-rating radio station I'd have to lug him, over my shoulder, up two flights of stairs.

I greeted Larry with as much warmth as I could muster, wheeled him to my car and stowed his luggage.

Larry Adler, a former *Oldie* columnist, at The Oldie of the Year Awards in 1993

Once, when we were running late for an on-air interview, he broke into a kind of canter and then, at my urging, a gallop. He was a pro. He was fun

Then he rose, gave the young girl an avuncular peck on the cheek and slipped into the back seat.

A miracle!

Larry was able to walk perfectly well. No doubt he could do the rumba if required. Once, when we were running late for an on-air interview, he broke into a kind of canter and then, at my urging, a gallop. He was a pro. He was fun. And he had endless stories about the famous. But he never told the tale of the miracle.

Three days later and it was time to say goodbye. At the airport again he got out of the car and said: 'Would you ask them for a wheelchair. Say I can't walk without pain.' In the Qantas Golden Wing lounge – I had talked our way in, following Larry's suggestion – I raised a glass to him. The last I saw of Larry he was waving farewell over his shoulder, the first passenger on the plane home.

Attended, of course, and in his customary wheelchair.

© The Oldie Magazine

Peter Golding

In my early days I was in the local Willesden 27th Boy's Scouts which became a superb grounding for later years and there were two senior scouts who played in the troop's shows and camp fires. One played the guitar and the other played the harmonica and I got hooked on both instruments.

My mother, who I love to this day for it, took me to buy a Hohner 270 chromatic harmonica and every lunch time I would cycle home from school to spend half an hour playing. I loved Folk Music and Jazz and would perform in youth clubs playing campsite songs and some blues and jazz numbers as well.

I recall that there was a Vaughan Williams concert on the radio with Larry Adler performing which I made a point of listening to on the radio in the kitchen. Larry was the first to become of senior importance to me and no doubt to many others on the instrument.

I then had the opportunity to meet Larry on a Hohner stand at an exhibition (possibly Olympia) and by coincidence, it just happened that I had become friends with Peter Adler around the mid 1970's. Peter and I were in the same social group so when I met Larry, there was already that connection. I remember I also was invited by Peter, with a group of his friends, to Larry's 75th Anniversary celebration in 1989 at the Royal Albert Hall. When Larry played a duet with Gershwin's piano roll (I think *Rhapsody in Blue*) with the empty piano notes playing. Quite an enthralling moment!

Peter Adler always referred to his dad as Larry and it was Peter, who later invited me to perform at Larry's memorial concert. I was introduced by Jonathan Shalit (who had been Larry's agent) as a 'family friend of both father and son'.

I was by then a London fashion designer, travelling to the Far East - places like Hong Kong - and music was my passion rather than my first thing although I always took the opportunity to play there with the local bands when I could and by that time, on the blues harmonica Marine Band too.

I came across the *America Harmonica News*, a monthly publication that introduced me to all the harmonica news and players from the USA. I decided to make a CD called *Stretching the Blues* which was then released by Indigo Records. For its grand release I invited many people and that included Larry who came along with his partner Gloria. Of course, Peter Adler was also there. The event was effectively 'Fashion meeting the Blues'. Peter Golding, Stretch Jeans, with 500 of my 'best friends' at the Café de Paris!! It was an indulgence but it was something I was very pleased to do. White/Black Rock 'n Roll jackets with a full great band line up plus special guest musician pals including Slim Jim Phantom, Otis Grand, Doris Troy, Leo Sayer and Kid Creole…!

Larry was filmed and interviewed at the release and asked if he was pleased to be there. "Yes" he replied. Do you like the music? "Yes" he replied. What do you think of Peter, is

Peter Golding © Portrait by Italiaander

he a good harmonica player? "Umhhh"! Surely you have room to talk about other harmonica players? "Look" said Larry. "Peter may be a very nice boy... but there's only one harmonica player in the world… and that's me"! He said this with his well known, cheeky smile and of course, he was

Harmonica's Grand Centurion by Rob Paparozzi

When Larry Adler picked up his first chromatic around 1926, you can only imagine what it felt like. Young Larry never looked back. He had no mentor on this instrument so he pioneered and stretched its limitations, taking it into genres and styles that the instrument was never even built for. When he ran away to New York, my guess is he had a plan, to show the world that this little toy had a much bigger place in the world of Music.

NYC is a tuff town with a talent pool large enough to drown in. When I played my harmonica in the 90s on Broadway at the legendary Palace Theatre I would often wonder about Larry Adler playing on that very stage for Mr Ziegfeld in the Follies, when he first got into town aged 16! NYC was the musical capital of the world at that time for recordings, classical music at Carnegie Hall and the top composers, such as the Gershwin Brothers and The Duke Ellington Band. Imagine the confidence he possessed just diving into the musical abyss of this city. Singlehandedly, Adler demanded respect for the instrument on Broadway, Concert Halls, Recording Studios and in the Movies and dared the Musicians' Union Local 802 to allow it a place in their listings and him to become a member. Trips to Hollywood and London brought world fame for Adler and the harmonica, and the 10 HARMONICA WORLD Feb/March 2014 most famous composers started writing pieces for him. Blacklisted in the US, he returned to live in the UK. It amazes me that his self-taught skills were enough to compose an Oscar nominated score for *Genevieve* in 1953.

Fast forward to around 1975. I had already been playing harmonica since 1966, playing along with John Lennon and Paul Butterfield recordings. I had never heard of Larry Adler until one morning my mom asked me if I was serious about playing my little harmonica. She asked if I'd ever heard of Larry Adler. I told mom, no. She said, Sit down and I will read you today's story on him in the NY Times. I was mesmerized as she told me about his career and that the following night would be his first show in the US since he left in the 1950s. The show was at the esteemed Rainbow Grill. I went to the show, met him and shook his hand. I realized on my train ride home how little I knew about the instrument I was now so fond of.

I knew that day that Blues Harp was just one of the things I loved. In 2009, I won the prestigious Bernie Bray Award at SPAH. I surely thanked John Lennon and Paul Butterfield and Toots but owed it all to that handshake with Larry Adler...

Thank you for the music, and the respect you fought for, for all of us, Happy Centenary, Mr Adler - we miss you!

When Harry met Larry by Harry Pitch

I got my first mouthorgan in 1933 and it was not very long before I had a repertoire of popular tunes but I could not play everything!

Larry Adler had just arrived from America and was performing on the London stage. When I saw pictures of him and heard him on the radio, I realised that his mouthorgan had a button on the side, giving more notes than I had. The salesman in our local music shop showed me what he was using and what the chromatic could do and I got one on my next birthday.

I soon became proficient on it and joined a harmonica band that played at concerts in the London area. Hohner organised National Championships and our band entered. We won first prize in the London Championship, and I got the prize for the best soloist. The prizes were presented by Larry.

When I received mine he told me I reminded him of himself when he was my age and won his first award. This was 1938 and Larry was an inspiration to all young harmonica players at the time.

Going forward several years, I was booked to play in Pizza Express' jazz venues. When I played at their Chalk Farm restaurant, Larry would come down and sit with my wife, Ruby. She found that he was pleasant and friendly, and, far from being a name dropper, he did actually know all these film stars.

A Chance Meeting with Larry – Cindy Lass

It was an unexpected meeting on a narrow path leading into my new tennis club. An oldish man stopped to let me pass. He started talking to me and was very charming and funny at the same time. I didn't want to be late for my match and as I said goodbye he told me that I owed him money for entertaining me. I replied that he owed me more as I was 'hot' and looking fab in my short white tennis skirt, with long tanned legs. He laughed and introduced himself as Larry Adler. I had never heard of him and had no idea he was the greatest mouthorgan artist in the world!

Later on he explained he always says hello and his name, telling me to never assume that people know who you are! That was the beginning of a beautiful friendship from his 80th year to his death at 87. After a couple of weeks, I just knew how life changing and important his friendship would be to me; I just felt it. He saw me, Cindy as a woman and artist rather than wife or mother. He was a true, honest, kind and genuine friend. It was a fabulous friendship. He was always talking about playing tennis with Charlie Chaplin and all the great film stars such as Cary Grant that he knew. After that fleeting meeting, I bumped into him with his good mate Victor Lownes. They played tennis for hours and chatted even longer - a compliment to Victor as Larry's brain was as sharp and as quick as a fiddle. I never saw him as an" old man" again!

I am a self-taught artist; I did my first painting for my mum in March 1994 and didn't look back. The reason I am telling you this is that on this day I had just finished doing 40 walk out first but he said that was rude. I realized then, that Larry's hearing must have been so acute and, if something was out of tune, it obviously hurt him. I didn't know whether he meant Leo or the piano or both? Another morning, Larry said he'd pick me up in an hour and was that ok? When the car pulled up outside a mansion block in Kensington, I never asked why or where we were going. I knew I might hear Larry play and that was sufficient. We entered a penthouse on a split level. A guy was playing madly on a piano and it turned out to be David Helfgott. I hung back and watched as Larry stood beside him and started to play; IT WAS MAGICAL.

I hadn't seen the film *'Shine'* which was David Hefgott's story. The next day, Larry was with a similar crowd and was invited in the evening to George Street, W1 to a private house; Larry had put his mouthorgan in his pocket knowing DAVID would be there playing and said if he felt like it, he might play as well.

Larry was a dear and loyal friend. I had hung my paintings in The Halcyon Hotel, Holland Park where one of the regulars was Michael Winner. I had a run in with him but as I stood my own ground, he then said something not kind about me. Bless him, Larry had an article going out in 'Boz' magazine and he mentioned this in a light hearted way - his comments at the same time sticking up for me. Larry believed in justice, even if it wasn't someone he knew that well. He was a brilliant letter writer. One night Larry and I were having dinner at Weng Wah House restaurant and he showed me a letter from an artist in the USA who had dated the sculpture that she had made of Larry. The date was my birth date and I was really excited about this. Larry wanted me to ring the lawyer, who lived in flat under the artist, and get it shipped over. So I rang him up but he wanted money, saying that the artist owed him back rent and she had left a few of her works to him. I said; "I'm not sure Larry understood there was money involved". I asked how much and he said $3,000. I was going to New York anyway so I arranged to purchase it, collecting it from the Mercier hotel lobby. The next question was tricky. You see I had to work quickly as Larry's 85th birthday was approaching and he really wanted it on stage whilst he played at the Queen Elizabeth Hall. I told Larry that I could get it but that he wanted money. "Oh" he said. "Larry, don't worry I will get it; However, should I ask your children first if they are interested to do so"? As they were not interested in acquiring it, I decided that I would get it. When I met the lawyer in the New York hotel and saw the sculpture, I jumped for joy in the darkened lobby and felt such happiness. It was then shipped back to the UK.

At this time, I was pregnant with Oliver and my gynaecologist had told me, if the baby hadn't moved for 4 hours then I needed to go in and check all was ok. Sitting in Larry's concert with the bust of Larry shining out on stage, when Larry started to play little Oliver bounced around till Larry stopped. Oh how proud Larry would be to know he's a fantastic guitar play with a real ear for music. Larry was adorable with him.

Today, while completing the writing of this, Larry would have been 100 - 10th February 2014. Dear Gary, who Larry introduced me to, suggested that we meet this morning at Hoop Lane Cemetery in Golders Green where Larry's funeral service took place. I finally saw Larry's memorial plaque. As I looked into Gary's kind eyes I felt Larry there, with us.

Thank you so much for doing this tribute book Gary - Larry would love it!

Cindy Lass, Cindy Lass
I've said it before, you're a pain in the ass
Your paintings are happy, they fill me with glee
But I don't like you being more famous than me
I'm well-known in Thailand, I'm famous in Siam
But in England your getting more famous than I am
One great female painter is Rosa Bonheur
But now you are getting more famous than heur
So Cindy Lass, Cindy Lass
You're a pain in the ass, you're a snake in the grass
But I love you to bits cos you've very nice tits
But you'll have to give up this publicity blitz
So I leave you with this, my adorable Cindy
The blast from your fame's getting too goddam windy

To Cindy
Rembrandt
van
Adler

Larry's Final Resting Place

While working on this tribute, I constantly had the date 10th February 2014 in my mind; the date of Larry's birth 100 years on. It seemed like the ideal day to visit his final resting place, Golders Green Cemetery. Although I've been there before I felt drawn that day, and it provided the opportunity to photograph the commemorative plaque which has been placed there (amongst a number of other well-known names).

On my arrival at the cemetery, I thought it best to check with the office administration that I had permission to take photographs for this book. The person in charge, a lady called Christine, was extremely forthcoming, though she specified that I would need Larry's family to give consent first. I explained about their awareness and contributions to this project and that I didn't think it would be a problem.

At that instant, my phone buzzed as it received a text. Much to my astonishment it was from Larry's daughter, Marmoset,

Larry's final place of rest ...

But his music lives on ...

Obituaries ...

OPINION & FEATURES

What a mouth!

News 9

Adler, king of the harmonica, dies aged 87

How I loved Ingrid Bergman and survived Hollywood's blacklist by Larry Adler

NEWS 27

Adler, king of the harmonica, dies

LARRY ADLER

A tribute to Larry Adler, the legendary harmonica player, who has died

The royal jester who dumped Ingrid Bergman

by Glenys Roberts

6 OBITUARIE

Larry Adler

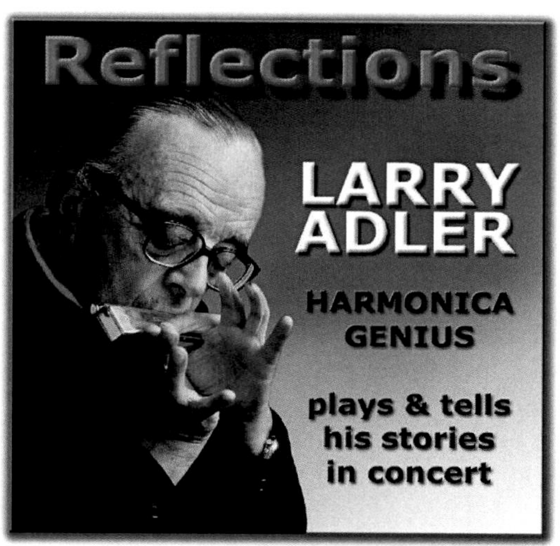

Reflections Larry Adler Harmonica Genius – Plays and tells his stories in concert. A superlative album, featuring outstanding masterful performances by Larry Adler (and entertaining and insightful anecdotes regarding Larry's experiences with some of the most famous names in entertainment history). Available to download from major online music retailers.

The magnificent classic tracks include: *Summertime, Our Love Is Here To Stay, My Funny Valentine, Sophisticated Lady, Begin The Beguine, Minuet In G. Opus. 167, Wedding Dance From Symphonic Suite 'Hasseneh'*.

And Larry recounts his experiences with Duke Ellington, Guy Lombardo, Billy Holliday, Maurice Ravel (*Bolero*), George and Ira Gershwin *(Rhapsody In Blue),* Ingrid Bergman (*Gettysburg Address and Battle Hymn Of The Republic*), June Allyson and Margaret O'Brien (*Clair De Lune*); introduces *Bess You Is My Woman Now,* and speaks about *Hollywood and the Blacklist, Genevieve, Larry Makes It At Last and The World Discovers Larry Adler!*

© Portraits by Italiaander

www.italiaander.co.uk